I0583577

HIDE

HIDE

AZOPHI ACADEMY™ BOOK THREE

TR CAMERON   MICHAEL ANDERLE   MARTHA CARR

DISRUPTIVE IMAGINATION

This book is a work of fiction. All of the characters, organizations, and events portrayed in this novel are either products of the author's imagination or are used fictitiously. Sometimes both.

Copyright © LMBPN Publishing
Cover by Mihaela Voicu http://www.mihaelavoicu.com/
Cover copyright © LMBPN Publishing
A Michael Anderle Production

LMBPN Publishing supports the right to free expression and the value of copyright. The purpose of copyright is to encourage writers and artists to produce the creative works that enrich our culture.

The distribution of this book without permission is a theft of the author's intellectual property. If you would like permission to use material from the book (other than for review purposes), please contact support@lmbpn.com. Thank you for your support of the author's rights.

LMBPN Publishing
PMB 196, 2540 South Maryland Pkwy
Las Vegas, NV 89109

First US edition, October, 2020
ebook ISBN: 978-1-64971-192-2
Print ISBN: 978-1-64971-193-9

For those who seek wonder around every corner and in each turning page. And, as always, for Dylan and Laurel.

— T.R. Cameron

THE HIDE TEAM

Thanks to our JIT Readers

Veronica Stephan-Miller
Diane L. Smith
Dave Hicks
James Caplan
Kelly O'Donnell
Kerry Mortimer
Jackey Hankard-Brodie
Deb Mader
Larry Omans
Paul Westman

Editor

SkyHunter Editing Team

CHAPTER ONE

The computerized voice rang through the *Cronus*'s corridors, echoing the one he'd heard through his comm thirty seconds before. "Set Condition One throughout the ship. Drop shuttles cleared for immediate launch." UCCA Special Forces Captain Jackson Reese pelted toward the hangar that held his transport and his team while running through diagnostics in his helmet display to ensure his drop suit was fully operational for the mission ahead. His body dodged members of the *Cronus*'s crew without conscious instruction.

The hangar was a large rectangle with ships along the walls and an exit hatch positioned in the center of the floor. When the captain set the ship to its highest combat state, as it was now, vacuum filled the space to allow the craft held within to depart without constantly cycling atmosphere. He paused at the bulkhead door and watched as a black shuttle exited. The entrance opened at his command the instant the hatch was secure and closed automatically a second after he passed through.

His black shuttle was on the far wall, and he sprinted toward it at his top speed. As he neared the opening at the stern of the squat, boxy vessel, his people came into view. His display checked off his team members by placing a set of initials in the air above each helmeted figure. This would be their last mission together for an unknown amount of time, and it had kicked off a full hour earlier than planned, thanks to the unexpected arrival of several Confederacy battleships.

Beatrice "Wasp" O'Leary would take charge of the team while he was officially on leave, and unofficially on detached duty investigating a matter important to both the Special Forces and Azophi Academy. The thought of the castle in Scotland filled with high-fliers looking to take the next step forward brought a smile to his face, and he would have been hard-pressed to deny it was largely because that's where Dr. Juno Cray made her home. She hadn't yet requested a second date, but he was sure she would. *Pretty sure. It's likely, anyway.*

The Artificial Intelligence that had finished its integration with his brain over the previous weeks made a noise that resembled a laugh. *Shut up, no one asked you.* Athena had proven to be far more sarcastic than he'd ever imagined a computer could be. But at least ten times a day, he wondered if he should have let the mission fail rather than have her implanted in his skull. At the time, it had seemed like a good idea.

Across from Wasp was Darius "Dare" Lyton and beside him Kyra "Books" Venn. The fourth and newest member of the team, Sebastian "Strings" Welker, was in the furthest seat. *But when I leave, there will be a new newest member.* He had every faith in Wasp's ability to lead his team, but that still didn't make it easy to step away, not by a long shot. And, since she'd probably move on to head a different squad when he returned, this would be his final mission with his most capable subordinate. She shifted aside so he could take the spot closest to the door.

Jax sat and grabbed the harness straps while announcing, "Stick, button up and let's get the hell out of here." An affirmative sounded from the pilot's cabin, and he called up an exterior view on the display to watch the shuttle door close. Athena had quickly learned to integrate with his drop gear, and she populated his visual field with essential data. The bow-mounted camera was in one small square, vital sign information for each of his team members in another, and an external view of the space surrounding the *Cronus* in a larger one that took up a third of the available area.

Within its boundaries were eight capital ships and a host of smaller craft that flitted around them like furious wasps. Beams of energy connected one ship to the next on an almost constant basis, and torpedoes and projectile weapons increased the danger. He scowled and added unnecessarily, "And try not to get us shot down, okay?"

The pilot's curse in response was inventive and appropriate and made him smile for the first time since the alarm went up. O'Leary asked, "So why the scramble?"

Jax shrugged. "Recon suggested the system wasn't defended, only the planet, so we should have been able to drop secretly and soften up the target as usual. Turns out recon sucks."

His team laughed at that, and Venn replied, "Far from the first time. They should hand that job over to SF."

"We're too busy to undertake that responsibility. And we can't lower our standards to add recon people, right? I mean, we're already scraping the bottom of the barrel with Strings over there." Again, laughter came, but it was good-natured. A team rule was that no one was allowed to take offense at being made fun of, including him. *Another reason I'll miss Wasp. She has the best insults.* "Anyway, that's the deal. Once we spotted the Confederacy ships, ours jumped in to keep the other side distracted while the *Cronus* delivers us to the target."

Lyton stated the obvious. "That doesn't really explain why we're bugging out." The shuttle lifted and headed for the hatch in the center of the bay.

"Yeah. Turns out that we didn't manage to distract them all, and one of the big ships is after the *Cronus*. So, to make sure we're not here if it goes wrong, we're heading out a little early."

O'Leary sighed and observed happily, "Just another day in the Special Forces."

Fate decided that such a tempting offer couldn't stand without a response. The shuttle jerked suddenly, then began evasive maneuvers. The erratic moves threw them all against the harnesses that saved them from smashing into each other and the ship's bulkheads. His external view showed a quartet of fighters chasing them. While their vessel could evade capital ships' fire reasonably well, it had little chance of escaping the smaller craft despite Stick's impressive piloting skills.

The yellow light that indicated imminent jump appeared on his display. *Stick must be too busy flying to talk. Not a good sign.* Jax called, "Everyone up, mag boots active, hold onto the rails. Double time." They swatted their harness releases and obeyed his commands, then yanked rifles from their holders on the bulkheads and shoved them into the protective cases positioned on the back of their jumpsuits. The light switched to green, and instead of retracting normally, the rear panel of the shuttle flew off, detached from the ship by a series of small charges. *Another really bad sign.* He shouted, "Everyone out," deactivated his mag boots, and jumped into space.

A blast struck the shuttle, and it caromed into his side and sent him spinning. Athena adjusted his display automatically to provide a static view of the exit he'd traversed. His people bailed in a surge and cleared the craft before the next hit. The AI plotted an inbound missile, and he shouted, "Stick, eject!"

The pilot had other ideas, and rather than immediately abandoning ship, instead wrenched it to the side to collide with a fighter that had gotten a little too aggressive. Explosions went off all around the shuttle, one of them the rocket-propelled escape pod that was the pilot's compartment flying free. It fell toward the planet below. Then Jax was out of time to worry about anything other than his plummet.

The fighters had lost sight of him and his team. Their small size, the shuttle's last maneuver's distraction, and their drop suits' electronically camouflaged surface provided adequate concealment. A shield powered by heavy backpacks hovered an inch beyond the suit's skin and absorbed the friction of their plunge into the atmosphere. Woven metal fabric connected arms to torso and spread between their legs to allow them all to get into proper position for the latter part of the drop.

The familiar rectangular wireframe pipe appeared in his display, and he steered into it. "Athena, what happened to the escape pod?"

The AI replied, "We are out of visual range. Its encoded beacon is still active. Also, you do not need to speak aloud for me to hear you." She loved pointing that out to him, to judge by the number of times she'd done so.

"Yeah, yeah, whatever." He activated line-of-sight communication with his unit. "All right, Athena says Stick's probably okay." It was an exaggeration, but the team could use a boost, and there was every possibility it was also accurate. "Focus on your landing. Since they know we're coming, we'll go to Plan B." Their usual approach was to try to penetrate an enemy facility separately, using stealth or disguise. That was far less viable when the bad guys were on the lookout.

Their suit computers directed them to the same landing zone, a clearing in a thick patch of trees. Despite being the first one out, he was the third to land. His parachute deployed at the proper moment, jerking him upward and providing the deeply uncomfortable sensation that his stomach had kept right on going without the rest of him. He landed cleanly and grabbed the lines as they split off from his suit to recover and bundle his chute. Less than five minutes later, they had all stripped out of their drop suits and left them carefully hidden under a tree at the edge of the clearing. It was standard practice where civilian presence was unknown to keep them out of sight. Anyone attempting to retrieve them who lacked the proper UCCA transponder would find them an impressively explosive surprise.

They'd opted for woodland camouflage since the trees provided cover right up to the edge of the town the Confederacy had selected as a base. Enemy forces had only been on the planet for a week, having taken it from the Alien Coalition in a brief but bloody struggle. The United Constitutional Corporate Alliance hoped to take it from them in turn and ideally put their time to better use in setting up stronger defenses. The Confederacy's slow buildup had struck him as a potential trap, but UCCA intelligence claimed supply chain issues were at fault.

Of course, that was the same organization that was engaged in some backdoor arms deal with a pirate group, and probably also had its fingers in the development of the Artificial Intelligence he'd stolen on Professor Maarsen's behalf. No one expected it would wind up in his head, nor that once it was in there, it would send out connective threads to ensure maximum efficiency—in Athena's words —and simultaneously make it impossible to remove without killing him, in Juno's estimation.

At the moment, none of that mattered. His team was kitted out in uniforms, body armor, helmets with transparent faceplates, and rifles in hand. Each of them also carried grenades and a pistol, although preferences differed. His gun was pure projectile, capable of shooting one explosive-tipped bullet at a time or a full magazine in under three seconds. His belt held grenades of lesser lethality: web, flashbang, and smoke. He nodded at the four faces staring at him. "Let's do this. Dare point, then me, Books, and Strings. Wasp, you have rearguard."

She scowled. "You're only putting me in back because this is your last chance to be a jerk to me."

Jax shook his head. "I'm completely certain I'll have many more opportunities before the mission's over. I'm doing it because I dislike you." His team laughed, and he grinned. "Let's go wreck some Confederacy troops' days. Move out."

CHAPTER TWO

They made it to within a kilometer of the city before Lyton's suit sensors detected trouble. Their gear communicated through line-of-sight data transfer, so as soon as one received useful information, it was instantly available to everyone. He didn't have to order the team to stop. They all froze automatically as the heat signatures appeared at the edge of their scanning range.

Dare said, "I make it four," and Books replied, "Four confirmed."

Jax delayed responding as he watched to see what the figures would do. It quickly became apparent that they'd stumbled on a patrol, and the foursome was headed in their direction. Two options presented themselves. Hide and wait for them to pass, and hope that their foes' ability to detect intruders was less effective than theirs. Or, take them out and hope they were only reporting in occasionally, and that his team would have some time before anyone noted the enemy patrol's absence.

He mostly defaulted to action in such situations, and this

sunny afternoon on planet Vermar was no different. "Dare and Books, circle right. Wasp, you and Strings circle in from the left. I'll go straight ahead. Keep the noise down. Low power stun to start." Projectiles and explosions could give them away. "But if they're armored or that doesn't work, do what you have to do. We can always use this as a diversion and go in on a different vector. Wasp kicks off the action." His instructions made it likely that she'd be the first to be in range since their targets were headed in that direction. Plus, she'd be smart enough to observe the team's positioning and make her decision on that basis. *And finally, it's one more chance for me to watch her in a leadership role and see if I can spot any problems.* He'd reviewed all her after-action reports in the previous weeks and had found nothing concerning. That didn't make his worry vanish, though. Major Anika Stephenson had patted him on the shoulder and told him that's what leadership was like. It would have sounded condescending from almost anyone else, but not from her.

Jax approached the quartet cautiously, stepping heel to toe in a slow walk and staying near the trees he passed. The trunks were three times larger than he could reach around and rose at least forty or fifty feet into the air. The broad leaves blended into a canopy that filtered the illumination coming in. *Of course, thermal detection doesn't care too much about that, and you have to assume that if we have it, they have it.*

He lowered himself to the ground and trained his rifle toward the approaching enemy soldiers. While there was no love lost between the fighters of each faction, neither was there any personal animosity. Jax and his team were professionals, and the others were the same, on a different side of the geopolitical divide. Where he could be nonlethal, he would be. Where he couldn't, he wouldn't lose sleep over it. Stephenson had discussed her philosophy on the matter over drinks with him one late night after a mission. "Jackson, it's simple for me. We all make our choices, and we live with their consequences."

So, here's hoping the consequences of our decisions turn out better than theirs. Wasp whispered, "Going on three," then counted up. When she reached the end, he pulled the trigger on the person in the front right of the enemy formation, which was a loose two-by-two. His audio pickups detected the electrical discharge of his team's weapons, and the yellow and red thermal body-shapes in his display fell. No fire came in response, so presumably, they'd been rendered unconscious. He stayed in position as Wasp ordered Dare to meet her at the bodies, then rose when she announced, "Clear."

The troops hadn't been armored, which he could understand given the ambient heat. He'd been sweating since peeling off the jumpsuit and was certain his team felt the same. Still, it was an odd choice since they should have received a warning from the fighters ahead of time, if not sooner. But it was possible the timing might have worked out such that this group was already patrolling. A swift search of the bodies revealed no additional information, so they secured the prisoners to one another with ties at their wrists and ankles, tossed their comms and weapons beyond easy reach, and moved on.

An indicator pulsed to announce the creation of a

private channel with O'Leary. "Something about this seem weird to you, Boss?"

"I was just thinking that. I mean, they might have already been out for a walkabout. But if they knew far enough in advance to reinforce with ships, how did that word not get down here?"

"Yeah. Like I said, weird."

"Keep an eye out, Wasp." He triggered the full team channel and warned the others to do the same, then added, "Let's vector to our right, in case someone noticed that little encounter." His squad reassembled itself into its former marching order and headed in the direction he'd indicated. They reached the edge of the trees without incident, and he peered ahead at the town, or at least what passed for one here. It was a collection of small buildings, none more than one story high. If they were arranged in any logical fashion, that mode of thinking wasn't one he'd previously come across. No grid, no wheel pattern, only a bunch of squat structures that looked like a giant had tossed them as if they were dice and they'd stayed where they stopped.

Jax shook his head and waved at the rest of them to crouch in the cover of the thick trunks and abundant leaves. "This looks even stranger from ground level." They'd discussed the oddness as they reviewed the recon materials from the spy satellite that had been inserted days before their arrival, and no one had been able to offer any reason at all behind it. "Let's launch a drone, Books."

A moment later, a new window opened in his display as the tiny aircraft climbed upward from their position. It was almost too small to see normally and had the same adaptive camouflage panels as the jumpsuits, which rendered it invisible. Even metal and heat detection failed to notice it. The one thing they'd found that *did* work was tracking the disruption it made in the air passing over it, but that was rather far afield from standard sensor practice.

It cycled through sensing modes every few seconds, from visual only, to sound, to thermal imaging. No results came back from outside the buildings, and the interior of the structures appeared equally vacant. "What the hell," he muttered under his breath.

Athena offered, "It appears the town is abandoned, Jax."

He rolled his eyes. *Yeah, it certainly does.* "All right, people. I'm open to suggestions here."

Venn sounded as confused as he was. "Doesn't make sense. Why would they put up such a fight up top after leaving the only city they'd claimed behind?"

Welker suggested, "Could the buildings interfere with the readings? Or electronic countermeasures set up inside them?"

Thinking back to a mission a few planets before, Jax added, "Maybe they have an underground complex that we missed."

O'Leary shook her head. "Possible but unlikely. I'm sure that's one of the first things the intelligence folks looked for with the satellite, and they had plenty of time on this one to do any checks they wanted to do."

Lyton shrugged. "So, are we agreed that it's a trap?"

Jax nodded. "Trap." Each of the others replied identically, including the voice in his head. "Damn, it's unanimous. Even Athena thinks so."

O'Leary laughed. "What's it like to finally be as smart as

the rest of us, boss? A whole new world for you, I'm guessing."

"Ha. That's a black mark on my report for taking such an easy shot. Aim higher, Wasp." He rose to his feet and patted the spots where his grenades, extra magazines, and pistol lived. Everything was in place. "Okay. We advance slow. I'm center, Wasp and Dare to my left, Strings and Books on the right. Outermost also protect our six. We stay together unless we need to break for cover, then you four go in pairs, and I'll be all heroic and hoof it on my own."

Venn snorted. "That's so you, boss."

"I know, right?" He inhaled deeply, then blew out his breath to center himself. "Game faces. Anyone pops up who's not us, put them down. If they don't show weapons, stun them, and we'll apologize later. If you sense danger, shoot to kill. Something's definitely not right here, and whatever game they're playing, it's up to us to knock over the table and punch them in the mouth for trying it."

They approached with rifles raised, moving with care but still covering the ground rapidly. They cleared the buildings as they came to them, with Lyton the designated door kicker and Venn sending the drone in to check for enemies or evidence. After the first couple, the process was irritating. When the fifth one revealed nothing of interest inside, Jax called a halt. *Athena, any connection to the* Cronus?

"Negative. The jamming continues unabated."

Damn it. "The *Cronus* is still unreachable. The fact that there's jamming is a good sign, means we haven't lost."

Strings countered, "And that we haven't won."

"Minus one point for negativity." He waved his hand as if making a mark on an imaginary chalkboard. "I see three options. One, we fade into the forest and watch and wait. Two, we keep doing what we're doing until we've cleared all the buildings. Three, we go inside them."

O'Leary replied, "Dislike the first, dislike the second, hate the third. If they did abandon this place, there's almost no chance they left without trapping it to hell and back. It's what we would do."

A squeal rang through their comms and caused Jax to bite his tongue hard enough to taste blood. A tinny voice wavered in and out of audibility as if its owner was screaming through a narrow metal pipe from the other side of the planet. He could only make out three words, "Reese," "Trap," and "Incoming." The way the others' rifles snapped up into guard position suggested they'd heard the same ones.

"What do you think about getting under cover now, Wasp?"

She growled, "I vote for the trees."

"Good plan. Run, people." They'd only managed about fifteen seconds of flight before ships screamed into view from above. Three transports about the size of their shuttle but hardened for landings in active combat zones headed for the town. One vectored to cut them off from the woods, another clearly intended to set down on the far side of the area, and the third appeared to have chosen the middle of the structures to touch down in. He yelled, "Faster. Maybe we can beat it." Getting caught with that ship between them and safety would be bad.

A UCCA fighter announced itself in a flurry of munitions and nailed the centermost transport with lasers and a missile. The enemy craft might have dealt with the first, but the second punched through the hull and detonated inside. It crashed into one of the buildings and exploded. The force wave knocked all of them from their feet.

As if the initial structure's destruction was a signal, every single other building in the town went up in simultaneous fireballs, which sent shrapnel and debris in all directions.

CHAPTER THREE

Jax wound up on his back, staring up at the bright sky. Everything seemed to be moving in slow motion as the portion of the debris that had been blown upward and outward from the surrounding buildings arced gracefully through the shafts of sunlight connecting heaven to Earth. *Oh, wait. I'm not on Earth. How did I wind up like this? Where am I? Apparently, a place with gravity, anyway, to judge by those large chunks of rock starting on their downward trajectory.*

Athena's voice was a shout that cut through the haze in his head. "Roll left, now." Her tone was urgent enough that his response was automatic, and he hurled himself sideways in a tumble. His brain came back online as he moved. *Oh, right, the Confederacy town.* She ordered, "Stop, pull in your legs." He did, and a huge block of foundation landed where his feet had been. "Now stand." He complied, and his right arm whipped out in a reflex strike to knock aside a piece of wood headed for his skull. That was faster than usual. He'd been working on increasing his proficiency with his prosthetic's amplified abilities but had never gone that fast. Finally, his mind caught up to the moment. *We're going to talk about that, Athena.*

"Survive first. Both transports have dispatched enemies. I've taken control of the drone through your helmet interface." A window opened on the right side of his visual display to show a view from high above. A group of eight moved in from the back of the town, relative to their entry point, and another squad of Confederacy troops advanced along the route he'd hoped to use for escape.

Jax growled, "Damn it. Incoming. Sound off and rally to me, people."

O'Leary's groan was the first to reach his ears. "Wasp." She stumbled up beside him and swayed a little. The others responded with varying amounts of vigor, and Venn had a hand on Lyton's shoulder to steady him. When they were all assembled, he ordered, "Stim," and pulled his dispenser from the med-pack on his belt. He stabbed the point through his uniform into his arm and depressed the button on the metal cylinder's top. Cold energy flowed into him as the stimulant raced through his body. His people noticeably straightened as they did the same. "All right. We're going after the ones in front of us and will use the transport as cover against the rest when they get here. We'll have to move fast." Assigning specific targets was unnecessary since when they chose one through their helmet's systems, the data would link to the other team members.

"Two by two, Venn with me in the front, Dare in the middle." Lyton still looked a little unsteady, so keeping him inside the formation would give him some extra time to react. "Switch to lethal options." No more stunning for this bunch. The stim had muffled his headache, but he still felt it creeping around the edges. *Athena, did I forget anything?*

"No. The enemies ahead are walking forward in an arc, presumably so you can't slip past them."

That's we, *Athena. You're one of us by default.*

The AI laughed softly. "I stand corrected. So we can't slip past them."

He nodded and regretted it as his brain banged around inside his skull. "Okay, move, people. Fast march, shoot as soon as you see something worth killing."

Jax kept his rifle pointed directly ahead and watched their approach to the enemy line in his display's birds-eye-view window. Limited cover was available since all the buildings had been reduced to rubble. He'd been carefully avoiding the stuff as he moved forward. The realization that his brain still wasn't working right hit him like a stun blast to the temple. He called, "Everyone down, prone behind anything that will shield you," and dashed ahead to a chunk of rock barely big enough to obscure his crouched form.

He'd figured the enemy might halt their advance since they surely had a high-level view of the action as well. But they kept coming and began firing at maximum range to force his team to keep their heads down. Simultaneously, they slowed their approach, and the reason for it couldn't have been clearer. "Damn them. They're delaying to let the ones behind us join in." His frustration blinded him for a moment, then he pushed it aside and refocused. "Okay, here's what we're going to do."

He didn't get to finish his thoughts before another occurrence dramatically shifted the playing field again. A

Special Forces transport rocketed into view at top speed, and Captain Catherine Lorenzo's voice sounded in his helmet. "We have the ones behind you, Axe." A string of black-clad bodies leapt from the ship as it skimmed near the ground. They hit and rolled several times before coming up with rifles pointed toward the enemy's position. He far preferred the high altitude insertion drops to those that carried so much risk of the shuttle being shot down on the way in, but the drop suits were designed to protect their wearers in either circumstance.

"Acknowledged, Valkyrie. Let's take it to them, team." He jumped up and ran while firing projectiles in full automatic mode. His magazine was empty in seconds, and he ejected it and switched to a new one on the run. The armor plates scattered over his body took several hits from energy blasts and bullets, one of which knocked him off balance. He turned the stumble into a forward roll and landed in a small depression. He grabbed the grenades on his belt and threw smoke and web in sequence although their foes were at the edge of his range.

Or, they had been, before adding his prosthetic arm to the mix. They arced to land behind the lead person on the left since his team's concentrated fire had already dropped the middle two. The webs covered them, and he shifted his aim to the ones not yet encumbered. The last three, having seen their comrades taken out while failing to do more than moderately injure his team, turned and ran for their ship. Jax pelted after them while calling, "Stun the webbed ones. We need to find out what the hell is going on here." He flicked his weapon to nonlethal, fired at the fleeing Confederacy troops, and dropped one. Presumably, some communication passed between them because one of the pair stopped and discharged a series of controlled bursts that forced Jax to juke and dodge, and slowed him down.

Venn sounded furious as she reported, "The webbed ones are dead. Shot from behind."

O'Leary snapped, "Bastards. Haven't they ever heard of loyalty?" She flashed past on his right. "Keep up, old man. I'll take the closer one out of your way."

He nodded and got himself moving again. "Strike two. First the lame insult, now this. I don't think much of your chances for promotion, Wasp." He groaned as a pain he'd noticed but hadn't paid attention to suddenly asserted itself. *Damn, cracked rib.*

Athena replied, "Probably broken."

Thanks for the pep talk, Coach. He ignored it and ran faster after throwing his heavy rifle aside, focused on covering the distance to his enemy. The vectors drew themselves in his mind, and he figured he had at least a fifty-fifty chance of catching his prey before he or she made it through the open back door of the transport. That calculation changed slightly as the vessel rose two feet off the ground and rotated to put its rear hatch right in the running soldier's path. *Bloody hell, I hate competent enemies.* It would be challenging but possible to get a grenade inside the thing, but he hadn't brought any explosives. *Idiot.* "Athena, can you do anything about the shuttle?"

"May I destroy the drone?"

He panted, "Absolutely. And yes, I know, I don't have to talk, shut it."

The combination of his damaged side and the distance he'd run slowed him down, and he feared he wouldn't be able to catch the other person. Then three things happened in quick succession. First, he saw a flash of light off the drone's metal wing as it turned off its camouflage and plummeted toward the front of the transport, right where the bow camera would be. Second, the pilot reacted to it, doubtless by reflex, and slewed the ship slightly. And that was enough to cause the fleeing soldier's jump to miss the rear hatch and bounce them off the vessel's side instead.

Jax arrived as his opponent returned to their feet, turned, and waved a fist at the shuttle climbing into the air. He called, "Let's settle down now. Your folks left you behind, and I have no desire to kill you."

The other person rotated to face him, and he saw a woman's face through the transparent shield. She triggered her external speakers. "You'll have to, or I'm going to kill you." She sidestepped toward her rifle, which had fallen on the ground beside her. He drew and fired his pistol in the same instant. The energy bolt blasted her weapon, scorched the surface, and rendered it unsafe to fire, at best. Still, she dove for it, snatched it up, and pulled the trigger.

Nothing happened. She snarled a curse and tossed it aside. "The fun way, then." She charged at Jax with a scream of fury, fists raised. He holstered his pistol and met her flurry of punches with a series of blocks.

"You're outnumbered. There's no chance you can win."

She threw a right hook that he blocked with his left. The reinforced knuckles of her gauntlet met the armor plate on his forearm. "I'm not in it to win it. I want to make sure you remember the fight." She spun and landed a kick on his damaged ribs, and he groaned.

Jax grumbled, "Okay, enough of that." She followed up

with a left hook, and he snapped his left arm out at full speed and broke her forearm. The blow carried sufficient velocity to break her balance and drop her to the ground. Beatrice O'Leary stepped into view and took her out with a stun blast. Jax shook his head. "How long have you been there?"

She shrugged. "Since she tried to shoot you and failed."

"And, what, you thought you'd watch?"

O'Leary laughed. "You said I wasn't doing well, so I thought I'd take the opportunity to learn from your example, oh wise one."

Jax couldn't contain his grin. "You'll fit right in with the other captains, Wasp. Now tie her up and let's drag her painfully through the town as we rejoin our comrades. If you see a piece of rubble, or maybe a long splinter, officially, you should avoid dragging her across it."

"Unofficially?"

"As squad leader, you'll face many difficult decisions. Consider this the first."

CHAPTER FOUR

With the town's destruction, the UCCA didn't bother locating its temporary base on that site. Instead, a shuttle picked up Jax and his team and took them a dozen miles away to a wide grassy expanse that provided excellent sightlines in all directions. The Special Forces weren't involved in the setup of planetary defenses, but he could picture a ship seeding the system with spy satellites, and another doing the same around the planet in a much thicker net. On the ground, four turrets sat atop four scaffolds, one at each corner of their perimeter. Workers busily reinforced the towers with structural metal plates that connected to a sunken foundation.

A temporary shield could be activated to protect the facility at need, but the batteries were still charging. Thus it was down at the moment and would stay that way until a threat appeared. The space between the corner defenses held an array of prefabricated buildings transported to the surface by cargo shuttles and assembled by workers, one pallet at a time. They would have used large containers with thrusters to handle the descent for big operations, but this was simply the initial fortress. The bigger stuff would allegedly come later. Jax had never stuck around long enough after an operation to see the construction of a permanent installation.

At the center lay a medical facility, and each of them had been treated for wounds absorbed during the fight. Mostly they'd taken damage from shrapnel, although a bullet had caught O'Leary in the shoulder. Wasp had laughed as the doctor dug it out and claimed she'd add it to her souvenir collection. Aside from Jax, she was the only one who required anything more than some surgical glue and painkillers.

Four rectangular buildings were positioned around the med center, two longer and two shorter. The former included a barracks and dining hall, and the latter an administrative building and security office with integrated prisoner lockup. Arrayed on the next layer outward were smaller structures like warehouses, tool shops, and other essentials for setting up and maintaining their foothold on the planet.

More of the small installations would be dropped strategically across the world, each with a limited force ready to defend their claim. The expense and logistics of it were undeniably staggering, but Jax didn't worry about it overly much. His part was done, save participating in some data collection. While he and his team would typically accomplish that task by searching through the stuff left behind by the enemy, in this case, the stones and splinters had very little to offer. So they'd have to rely on human intelligence, namely the soldier Wasp had taken down.

He strode forward into the shuttle landing zone, a space demarcated by a small fence. One of the *Cronus*'s standard shuttles filled the area inside that barrier, likely because his team's ride had been blasted to bits and left the Special Forces contingent one short. His first act when he'd regained contact with the ship had been to confirm that his pilot had survived, and he met the news that she had with great relief. He'd received that information directly from the woman stepping from the shuttle, Major Anika Stephenson. Her short-cropped blonde hair ruffled a little in the breeze, but it wasn't long enough to get in her piercing eyes or block the strong lines of her face. She walked like the bodybuilder she was, all coiled power ready to burst.

"Welcome to Vermar, Major."

"Quite a place you have here, Jackson. How are the ribs?"

"Fine." He pointed at the security office. "Our guest is right this way. Need a stop anywhere first? Cup of coffee?"

She shook her head. "I've already had three pots of the stuff today. It's not often one of my squads gets their shuttle shot out from beneath them and another winds up corkscrewing around in space after a missile to the engines."

He nodded. "At least Captain Lorenzo made it down unscathed."

His superior officer snorted. "I guess twenty-four hours to repair is better than fifty for Frangilo's or needing an actual replacement for yours. Captain Jensen is not pleased with you for getting her shuttle destroyed, by the way."

Jax winced. The commander of the *Cronus* was not someone you wanted to make angry. "I'll be sure to apologize once I get back."

Stephenson shrugged. "She probably won't throw you out an airlock if you do, but the odds are better than if you don't. You might want to carry air and a helmet with you for a while, though." Her deadpan expression gave no clue whether she was joking or not. "Any progress on our prisoner?"

They strode side by side along the narrow lane between the med center and the barracks, but barely. It was a good defensive design but less effective where comfort was concerned. The buildings themselves were a bland grey mix of modular metal and plastic pieces. "Her arm's been tended to, although we didn't give her any painkillers for it beyond the minimum needed during the procedure. Doc says the quick heal drugs will probably take a day to fix it. It took a lot of damage." The words came out flat and emotionless. He wasn't proud of hurting the other person, but as Stephenson had affirmed, choices had consequences.

His wrist comm transponder opened the outer door, and they stepped into a darkened control center. Displays clustered around the near corner showed views from cameras mounted on the turrets and feeds from the satellites flying overhead. Several also showed the swooping movements of a drone in terrain-following mode. The autonomous guards randomly darted around an extended perimeter as a backup to the humans tasked with the same responsibility. The operator was deeply engrossed in his work and spoke quietly with someone over his headset comm.

Jax took Stephenson to the back wall, where two doors led to separate incarceration-slash-interrogation spaces. Entry required his transponder and a security code tapped into a pad, and he stepped through first to ensure that the prisoner wasn't waiting to spring upon them. She sat idly on the solid platform that served as the room's only furniture. She looked up at their entrance and scowled. "You again. Here to break the other arm?"

Jax shook his head and secured the door behind his boss as she crossed the threshold. "Not unless you force me to. I told you to stand down. You didn't listen."

"Would you have in my place?"

"Yes." A soft snort sounded from the AI in his brain, who had gotten entirely too comfortable with her role as his inner critic. *Shut up, you. I might have. It's possible.* "But that doesn't matter. Allow me to introduce Major Stephenson. She has a few questions for you."

The woman shifted her gaze to Stephenson. "You're his boss?" She nodded. "My condolences."

Stephenson barked a laugh and shook her head. "You seem to have a way with women, Captain. But it doesn't appear to be a *good* way." She turned her attention to their prisoner. "Name and rank, please."

"Kendrick, Hayley. Lieutenant."

The Major crossed her arms and stared down at the other woman. Their captive was dirty and disheveled, but still retained a fighting spirit that Jax recognized from his people and himself. She might not be the Confederacy equivalent of Special Forces, but she was undeniably a warrior at heart. Her blonde hair was shaved almost to the skin on the sides and back of her head and was short and spiky on top. Thin lips and narrow eyes gave her a stern look. "Well, Kendrick, Hayley, care to explain what you and your team were up to today?"

She grimaced. "Not really. I think my superiors would frown on that."

Stephenson nodded. "That's completely understandable, and likely the same answer I would give in your situation. However, I don't believe you fully understand what's going on. Allow me to explain." She turned to face him. "Captain, some of this will be new to you as well." She walked to the corner of the room and leaned back against it, presumably so she could easily see both of them. "It turns out that this particular operation was absolutely screwed from the get-go. Our incursion force, which showed up expecting to find nothing in the system based on recon done almost immediately before, instead found a ton of capital ships waiting for us."

She punctuated her words with gestures that he read as a mix of actual anger and an effort to push their prisoner's buttons. "So, clearly there was an information leak there. Let's call that problem number one. Then, when we get to our objective, the strangely under-defended Confederacy home base on Vermar, not only is it abandoned, but it's trapped. We'll refer to that as problem number two." She strode forward to stand over the other woman, who remained seated and stared upward. "And then your team shows up and tries to kill mine. We'll call that problem number three. And lest there be any confusion, problem number three makes me want to break your other arm on general principles."

Kendrick swallowed with an effort. "That's understandable, Major. I'm sure you understand it was nothing personal."

Stephenson, who had turned her back to return to her corner, spun and pointed. "See, that's the thing. It seems *very* personal. It seems as if the whole thing was a trap. And I'm very interested in knowing who it was intended to ensnare, or given the available evidence, to kill." She shook her head. "But we're still not at the most relevant part of the discussion where you're concerned. We just got word that UCCA intelligence is on the way to interview you." The prisoner paled suddenly, and Stephenson nodded. "That's right. You could expect decent treatment from the military under the standard rules of warfare, which no doubt made resisting our inquiries seem like a viable option. But if you're still in this room when they arrive, you're going into a black bag, onto a ship that officially doesn't exist, to be taken to an installation that's so secret it's set up to self-destruct rather than have a hint of its existence sneak out."

She folded her arms and stared at the prisoner. Kendrick's eyes were locked on the floor as she slowly shook her head. Jax wondered if she realized she was doing it. Her limbs trembled, seemingly at random. In her place, Jax would spill every detail he knew, although his clearance was almost certainly much higher than hers. Finally, Kendrick looked up. "What do you want to know?"

Stephenson grinned. "Everything. From the first moment you heard about this mission until you were stunned unconscious. Every single detail. And if I suspect for even a second that you've held something back, I walk out and leave you here until the ghosts arrive and take you away on their non-existent ship."

She nodded and cleared her throat. "May I at least have a glass of water? There's a lot to tell."

CHAPTER FIVE

After dinner was complete, the dining hall transformed into an officer's club by virtue of a rollaway bar being rolled into view. You made your own, or more often whoever was around took turns playing bartender. Jax always enjoyed the feel of being behind the counter, or in this case, oversized cart. But tonight he was only making drinks for his people, and Beatrice O'Leary helped him carry them back to the spot they'd claimed.

She sat beside him, with the other three on the opposite side of the long cafeteria table. O'Leary was strong, smart, and attractive. Rigorous discipline and enemy fire had burned away any hint of immaturity or unprofessionalism during the time he'd known her. He lifted his gin and tonic in a toast. "To Wasp. May she be twice the leader I am."

Sebastian "Strings" Welker snorted. "Hopefully she can aim higher than that, boss." Their newest member had only recently joined in the constant bantering insults they all traded. While his comments weren't all that original, his sense of timing was impeccable. Tall, thin, and fastidious,

Welker upped the sophistication level of the group considerably.

Darius "Dare" Lyton nodded in agreement. "Seriously. Like, she'd have to go backward to accomplish that." He was the most physically capable of the group, his dark skin stretched by his muscular form.

Jax shook his head. "You people are terrible. This is supposed to be a celebration, not a chance to pile insults on me before I wander off into the temporary sunset. Don't forget. Eventually, I'll be back, and you won't have Wasp to protect you."

O'Leary grinned. "No worries. I'll still have your sixes, no matter where I am."

Kyra "Books" Venn laughed. "Besides, boss, trashing you *is* how we celebrate." She raised her glass, straight bourbon over ice, and toasted, "To Axe. May he stay away long enough that we actually miss him for once."

He winced and put a hand on his chest as the team cackled at him. "You wound me. Deep inside, I'm terribly wounded. My heart bleeds."

Venn quipped, "Maybe you should get that replaced, too."

"Ow. Low blow, Books. Even by your standards." The others gave her a quiet round of applause. He replied wistfully, "I think I'll miss you least of all." They caught the reference since the *Wizard of Oz* had played on the *Cronus* a while before and they'd watched it together.

As usual, it was O'Leary who pulled them back to seriousness. *Honestly, she's even more driven than I am.* Athena, who apparently didn't want to be left out of the insult fest, gave a small laugh. "Except you're a terrible driver." He frowned. *Not quite there yet, robot.* He was pretty sure that term was mildly offensive to her, and he wanted to ensure she was included in the other part of the game, too. No reply came, and he nodded in satisfaction.

O'Leary asked, "So, what did you find out from the prisoner? What's all this about?"

Jax sighed. "Well, it was kind of about me."

Laughter erupted. Venn kept on for almost thirty seconds after everyone else and finally had to make a visible effort to stop. She wiped her eyes and shook her head. A single strained sound escaped her lips, and she rose suddenly. "I think I'll refresh our drinks." She moved quickly away, and the choking sounds of her suppressed mirth faded slightly.

When they all stopped looking at her and met one another's eyes again, Welker shrugged. "You have to admit, that sounded, uh, a little paranoid and self-centered. You know, on the surface."

He nodded. "I'm aware. And believe me, I wish it weren't the case, but it appears that it is. The prisoner, one Lieutenant Hayley Kendrick, isn't far enough on the inside to know the whole picture, but she gave us some broad strokes. Apparently, the Confederacy is aware of and interested in my existence."

Venn returned, set bottles of beer in front of each of them, and reclaimed her seat. "So, you're saying they invaded the planet and committed a dozen capital ships or so all for you?"

He rolled his eyes dramatically. "Of course not. The planet part happened before they knew about me." The others laughed again, and he shook his head. "No, the attempt to take the system was righteous, as was the capital ship defense of it, at least from Kendrick's perspective. For what it's worth, Major Stephenson agrees."

O'Leary grunted. "Worth a lot."

"I share your opinion. Anyway, they did somehow know several things they shouldn't have. First, that I have an artificial intelligence banging around in my skull."

Athena's voice displayed her disapproval of his words. "I am not 'banging around.' Tightly integrated would be a better term. You could add disappointed by the lack of cerebral activity if you wanted to be accurate."

Ouch. He didn't reply but sensed smug satisfaction from the AI anyway. "Second, that I'm generally on the *Cronus.* More worrisome is that they might have been aware I was with the ship at this specific moment, which signals an even greater leak of information. Third, that the *Cronus* would be the first one in when we went to retake the planet. Fourth, and possibly most concerning of all, they knew when we were coming, since they were absent for the recon but present for the incursion."

O'Leary observed, "Someone somewhere is on the Confed payroll."

Welker lifted a hand and rocked it back and forth. "Maybe. Or they've cracked a communication network. Or they have excellent observational intelligence going on. Could be anything, really."

Jax nodded. "But I'd put my money on there being a compromised person in the mix, perhaps along with that other stuff. In any case, they specifically aimed the trap at me."

Lyton frowned. "Why not simply blast us with a fighter, then? Why the booby traps and the squads?"

He chuckled. "Stephenson asked that question in almost those exact words, although she had a couple of colorful descriptors in there as well. Basically, our side forced them deep into their backup plans. First option was the *Cronus*, but they failed because our ships were ready to back us up. Then it was blasting the shuttle, which they managed, but we still survived it. Captain Jensen had a hunch that they were paying too much attention to us, so she requested additional support. Our fighters took out theirs before they could get down to kill us. Only the heavy armor on the transport shuttles let them make it through the screen."

Wasp shook her head. "There's one thing I don't get."

Jax replied, "Only one? You're having a good brain day, then."

She smacked him with a backhand on the chest that echoed in the cavernous room and caused the few groups seated at other tables distant from theirs to look over. "So, the idea is that they want to kill you because you stole their property, is that it? Why is it such a big deal to them? Was it the only copy or something?"

"According to Athena, several backup versions exist." It had been one of the earliest discussions the AI and Stephenson had shared, using Jax as an intermediary. "The Major's theory is that they want to be sure the Alliance doesn't get the chance to reverse-engineer it and nullify their advantage."

Welker asked, "Is that something we're close to doing?"

Jax lifted his hands, palms up. "Your guess is as good as mine. The people at the Academy think they can do it, which is one reason I'm heading off on detached duty. I mean, leave. Heading off on leave." His team already knew the broad strokes of his plans.

O'Leary snorted. "Now that I know she was such a deep information source, I almost regret dragging her over every rock along our walk through the town." His team laughed at the memory of that image. At the moment, he'd felt like it was quite appropriate, and now, with the distance of time and perspective, couldn't see a reason to disagree with his initial assessment.

"She wouldn't talk until we threatened her with the UCCA intelligence folks, though. The fear of being black-bagged helped her overcome her resistance to sharing."

Lyton growled, "That'd sure as hell work on me. I've seen the ghosts a few times, and something about them gives me the creeps. I mean, they look like normal soldiers, but the eyes tell a different story."

O'Leary added, "Like they've gone so deep into the realm of evil that now it's their whole existence." The rest of the team stared at her. "What? I read books, you know. Sometimes even stories about demons and stuff. Excuse me for being a little poetic." She took a drink of her beer and shook her head with a small smile. "Besides, it's pretty damn accurate."

Venn and Welker proclaimed that they'd never met an intelligence agent that they knew of, and Jax said the same. In his case, though, it wasn't completely true. Once upon a time, he'd been interviewed by a low-level worker from the division. The man had called himself a talent scout and had told him that Jax popped up on their radar after a particularly impressive infiltration involving both stealth and disguise. To look at, the intelligence representative had been nothing special—a bureaucratic drone. But after only a couple of minutes, Jax's instincts had started warning him of danger, and by the end of the discussion, it seemed as if the room had filled with an invisibly oppressive presence. He'd intentionally fumbled the conversation and hadn't heard from them again.

He shrugged. "Well, fortunately, we're usually out of the picture before they're in it, or vice versa. I don't have any particular desire to run into any of those people either."

O'Leary sighed, then said, "One more toast. To our fearless leader. May he stay a step ahead of the enemies on his trail and be in heaven an hour before the devil knows he's dead." They clinked bottles, and although the tribute was an odd mishmash of pieces drawn from questionable sources, it still gave him a warm feeling in the pit of his stomach.

That lasted for all of five minutes before Captain Catherine Lorenzo burst into the room at a run. She received a lot of comments about her short stature but was one of the hardest-working people Jax had ever met. "Reese, Stephenson wants us, right the hell now."

CHAPTER SIX

Jax followed Lorenzo as quickly as possible, but she was already a dozen yards ahead by the time he made it through the door. Her brisk strides ate up the ground. They headed away from the side of the installation where the shuttles landed and toward the warehouses and other assorted necessary buildings.

She waved her hand at the panel on one of the storage structures and motioned him inside. He walked into the dark, and she slipped in behind him and closed the door. *What the actual hell?* She shoved him toward the corner, and his eyes adjusted enough along the way that he spotted Special Forces crates at their destination.

Lorenzo hissed, "You need to get into your drop suit. A ghost came down on the last shuttle, disguised as a normal troop. Stephenson left word to put you in hiding right quick if one showed up."

"Damn." The more appropriate and more vulgar curses stayed in his head where only Athena could hear them.

"What about the prisoner?" He knelt to unlatch the crate marked with the icon for drop gear.

"Already gone. It's like the Major is psychic or something. After you two finished your interview, she took the woman straight up to the *Cronus* for safekeeping. Didn't explain why, but it seems pretty obvious now."

Jax nodded as he pulled on the suit over his uniform. "She knows way more than she ever shows. You only have to play poker with her once to know that." He sat on the crate to pull on his boots, then stood and strapped on his equipment belt and holster. "What's the plan?"

Lorenzo had been staring down at her comm the whole time. "We have eyes on him. So far he's wandering around and getting the lay of the land. But eventually, we can be sure that he'll shift from passive to active searching, and he probably has a lot of toys that will help."

"Yeah, true."

"So, my part ends now that you're aware. I need to make myself obvious. There's a box with an encrypted comm rig in the back corner. Use it to link up with Stephenson and figure out your moves from here." She lifted a fist, and Jax bumped it with his.

"Thanks, Valkyrie. Stay safe."

"You too, Axe." He crouched in a crate's shelter as she stepped out into the night and closed the door behind her. A soft click sounded as he donned his helmet and latched it onto the drop suit's collar. His display came to life and turned the dark interior into something approaching early morning illumination. He found the crate easily and unpacked the encryption unit, heavy transmitter, and antenna. The team constantly trained with all their gear, assembling and disassembling it while wearing blindfolds. Being who they were, it was almost always a speed competition. He wasn't the fastest at setting up the comms. That honor went to Sebastian Welker's nimble fingers. But in under two minutes, he'd attached the pieces and initiated a search for a receiver.

As the systems negotiated, he asked, *Athena, do you have any way to splice into the base's security?*

"Standby, Jax." After a few moments of silence, she continued, "Yes. I have access. What is your desire?"

He snorted inwardly. *You're not the woman I want to hear those words from. Careful, or you'll make Juno jealous.*

"You assume that she is as entranced with you as you are with her. This seems...unlikely." The pause was enough to convey the fact that she was screwing with him.

Yeah, whatever. Find the ghost and put him in my display. Also, give me a map of the facility with a green dot for my location and a red one for his. A moment later, a view from a turret camera appeared in a window, and beneath it the schematic of the UCCA base with two colored spots. The ghost had short brown hair, standard fatigues, and seemed to have an instinct for keeping his face away from the camera. His gait suggested strength and speed, but not too much of either. *Overall, average, like a good intelligence agent should be.*

He was near the barracks, not close enough to pose an immediate threat. Jax ordered his suit to dampen his heat signature to match the room temperature so thermal imaging wouldn't spot him, and sat so movement tracking wouldn't detect him. It was impossible to know what sort of tech the man might be carrying, and he presumed that was the reason behind the order to get into the outfit in the first place. *Athena, keep an eye on him and warn me if he seems like he's interested in this building.* His audio feed crackled to life. "*Cronus* comm."

"Reese, Jackson, for Major Stephenson. Urgent."

"Acknowledged. Standby." About forty seconds went by before his superior officer's voice, remarkably reassuring, sounded.

"Jackson. Status."

He watched the dot's progress as he replied, "Lorenzo thinks you're psychic. There's a ghost on site."

"Damn it."

"Concur. He's not here for the prisoner, is he?"

She sighed. "We don't think so. I've been exchanging messages with Maarsen. One of his people raised a flag that an intelligence op has been initiated with you as the target. I found out as soon as I got back up here, and put Lorenzo and Frangilo on alert."

"But not me."

"Of course not. Couldn't have you unintentionally endangering the source. You needed to seem clueless if you encountered him. Fortunately, we spotted the agent before he spotted you."

Jax nodded. "Understood. Less than optimal, but necessary. So what's next?"

"Well, that's the question, isn't it? Hang on. I'm checking the transport schedule." He used the moment of silence to check on the ghost, who was now inside the dining hall. *Getting closer. Any indication it's with a purpose?*

Athena replied, "Negative. His movements are consistent with an initial exploration of the area."

Stephenson said, "Here's what we need to do. There's going to be a cargo transport landing outside the base around dawn tomorrow. A big one, filled with crates of food supplies, so it's refrigerated. You'll want to be on it when it heads back up."

He frowned. "Like, you're going to clear it with the pilot so I can ride along?"

She laughed. "When do we ever do things that way? No, you'll sneak into the back so we have complete deniability. 'Jackson Reese? Haven't seen him in days. Maybe he went walkabout.'"

Jax sighed. "I get it."

"Quit whining, Reese. This is what you're good at." The element of sincere scolding in her tone snapped him out of his partial daze.

"Right. I think my brain must have gotten jostled in the explosions. On course and on target, Major."

The sternness in her voice didn't fade, but she sounded satisfied. "Great. Now, find a spot to hide out for the night, get on the transport, and contact me when you're in the air."

Jax knelt to start disassembling the kit. "You got it, boss."

His initial instinct had been to stay in the warehouse, but in the ghost's place, that would be one of the first places he'd check. He crouched at the exit that faced the back of the camp, away from the intelligence agent, who was now inside the barracks. *Probably interviewing people by asking seemingly innocent questions to see who will give up something useful.* He shook his head. *This is a lot more fun from the other side. Athena, is there anywhere to hide outside the base, within visual sight of it? The cargo transport should land on this end, but it's not guaranteed.*

"I'm tapping into the satellites and retasking a camera. It appears there's a depression about a half-mile from your current position. There is also some evidence that an animal has used it as a home."

What kind of evidence?

"Bones. Large bones."

Outstanding. Give me a path and make sure the base's security systems don't notice me. The problem with temporary setups like this was that it forced them to rely more intensively on technology than a more well-established installation would. One person watching the sensors instead of two, for instance. It allowed the AI more latitude to subtly adjust the wireless feed from the cameras before it reached the displays. They'd have buried cables in a permanent facility, but this one wasn't there yet.

Between Athena's machinations and his suit's adaptive camouflage, he easily made it to the spot she'd indicated. The warning about potential predators was reinforced by discovering that the large bones she'd described, probably about the same size as the leg bone in a horse or cow, had been aggressively gnawed upon. *Any ideas on how to deal with curious animals?*

"I could use your suit's external speaker to send out a low volume sound wave. It should deter them from approaching."

What's the risk of detection?

"Against passive scanners, minimal. Against active scanners, highly probable."

He sighed. *Okay, let's go with that since it'll be less noticeable than shooting them. I'm going to close my eyes. Alert me immediately if anything or anyone gets near enough that I need to worry about it, or if the transport shows up early, or if the ghost heads this way. Otherwise, please wake me an hour before sunrise.*

"Sleep well, Jax."

Surprisingly, he did.

A soft song played in his head, and it took Jax several moments to realize it wasn't happening in a dream. He blinked and coughed. "Ugh, I hate sleeping in my helmet. Always makes my neck stiff."

Athena replied, "But safer than the alternative."

Yeah, probably shouldn't be talking out loud, either. What's our status?

"The transport is due to land in forty-seven minutes. The list of contents suggests it should take between thirty and fifty-five minutes to unload. They'll be carrying empty crates back, so you'll need to find a moment to sneak in and conceal yourself among them." Her tone held a slightly amused note.

You mean hide inside *one, you're just not saying so.*

"It's true, that might turn out to be the safest option. There's no way to know until you can get a view of the interior."

I can tell when you're laughing at me.

She chuckled. "You think so, do you? How quaint."

Jax shook his head and removed his helmet long enough to drink some water and eat a couple of protein bars from the survival kit he'd snagged before leaving the warehouse. He heard the transport before he saw it, and the deafening noise it made certainly seemed appropriate given its size, equally twice the length of a normal shuttle. He'd noticed it parked on the far end of the *Cronus*'s hangar any number of times, but hadn't paid any particular attention to it. Still, it was probably a standard model, and he had a basic familiarity with all UCCA craft, most of the Confederacy versions, and an alien ship or two as well. It occurred to him, somewhat belatedly, that he had a computer in his head. *Athena, do you have a schematic for that ship?*

"Of course, Jax."

He put his helmet back on and saw all the details about the shuttle, from tonnage to exact measurements to cargo capacity in pounds, kilograms, feet, and meters. *Okay, I could get used to this.*

Her voice was droll, which was an impressive feat in itself. "Finally, some appropriate appreciation."

He sighed and stayed low as the transport landed and a flood of people moved in to unload it. "Damn it," he muttered. "There's no way I'm going to get there in this." He crouched and removed the jumpsuit, then pushed it as far under the small lip of the depression as he could. *Mark this spot and let Lorenzo know about it once we're gone.*

"Do you think this is a wise idea?"

He shook his head. *No, but I certainly can't march up in*

my drop suit and avoid attracting notice. This way at least I'll blend in a little. Where's the ghost now?

"He's near the entrance to the refrigerated section of the dining hall."

Okay, so I won't be able to sneak into a crate at that end of the route. What's the timing like on the folks coming and going from the transport?

"Times vary from between ten and thirty seconds between people."

All right. Give me a heading that gets me to a hidden spot near the transport so I can run in. He already regretted ditching his helmet, but it would have been a dead giveaway to anyone who happened to look his way.

"Three hundred and twenty-two degrees from the direction you're facing."

He turned a little to his left and started walking normally, as if out for an early morning stroll. The light was still low enough and his distance far enough that he shouldn't attract attention. *Athena, you're still subverting the camera facing us, right?*

"Of course, Jax."

He made it to within fifteen feet of the transport without incident by circling to approach the side opposite the installation. In the interim, the ghost had moved nearer to the shuttle, as if he could sense his quarry was nearby. *Athena, I'll go on your mark. Be sure to account for anyone entering, leaving, and most of all the damned intelligence agent.*

"Standby. You will run straight at the shuttle, then pause before circling the back and entering."

Understood.

"Go."

He ran as quickly and quietly as he could while saying a small prayer to the Universe that no one would look the wrong way at the wrong moment. He stopped before reaching the side of the ship and crouched reflexively.

"Standby." A pause of three seconds, then, "Go."

He jogged along the side, then slowed to a walk before rounding the corner. He almost froze when he spotted the ghost, but the man's head faced away as he exchanged words with one of the people bringing boxes back to the ship. Jax ducked inside and hid behind a crate, silent and still as the next one was brought in and piled in front of it. The boxes were only stacked in ones and twos since there wouldn't be as many going back up as had been sent down. Jax took advantage of that situation to climb into the back corner and surround that position with two-high stacks, moving them in the gaps between returning crates. He climbed inside the protected single in the corner, strapped on the mask from the survival kit, and tested the oxygen flow. *Safe.* He frowned as he shivered and a thought crossed his mind. *Athena, Stephenson said refrigerated, not freezer, right?* Only silence came in reply. *Damn it, Athena. Remember, if I die, you die.*

The AI's laughter sounded in his ears, but she didn't speak. *Guess I'm in for an uncomfortable ride. But at least it's not to an intelligence detention center.*

CHAPTER SEVEN

The trip up from Vermar to the *Cronus* was an episode Jax planned never to think of again. He didn't freeze, but he was cold the entire time, colder than he could remember ever having been. *I'm sure it was worse during basic training, but one tends to forget those moments. Or block them out.*

The chime of the transport's skids meeting the metal deck signaled their arrival. There probably wouldn't be a rush to unload and reload, but it still made sense to get out before someone noticed him. He couldn't ignore the possibility that one or more intelligence agents were present on the *Cronus*, and he needed to keep moving to stay ahead of his pursuers.

Jax waited long enough to ensure that anyone waiting to unload would have had time to do so, then clambered out of his hiding spot. He was sore, half-frozen, and vacillated between annoyed and angry from minute to minute. He cleared a path toward the exit, moving crates as silently as he could. *Athena, can you access the ship's systems?*

"Only the ones your comm has privileges for. The firewalls are substantial. Given several hours, I could likely break them, but at some risk of discovery. Should I try?"

No, let's not make a scene. Check the hangar cameras, and if we're clear, go ahead and pop the hatch on this thing.

"You'll need to move your comm closer to the panel on the rear wall."

He obeyed, and moments later the back hatch released, rising only enough for him to roll out beneath it. He stood and stretched, and his joints popped since they finally had room to do so. *That sucked. Let's never do that again.* He stayed in the shuttle's concealment and considered his options, much like he'd done the entire way up from the surface. When he'd pinged her, Stephenson had said, "Find me when you get up here," so that was his goal. How he was going to achieve it while also trying to maintain a low profile was still murky.

Athena, can you change the identity transponder in my comm? Make me into someone else?

She sounded like the question was one of a long string of stupid things she'd been asked. "Yes. Who would you like to be?"

He shrugged, then a smile crooked his lips. *Let's go with Gene Pryor for a name, and have Gene be an intelligence officer.*

"Done."

Okay, good. Now, give me a path to the gym. I should be able to get a shower and snag some better clothes there.

Jax's first inclination had been to head straight to Stephenson, but he'd have drawn serious attention in his dirty fatigues. His second, to go to his quarters to clean up was so stupid that he was embarrassed it had crossed his mind. But the exercise facility, with its large unisex locker room and showers, was perfectly suited to his needs. He'd taken off his outer shirt on the way in, so now he looked like a dirty, sweaty crew member who wore combat trousers instead of standard ones. He'd wrapped his equipment belt and holster in the shirt.

The AI hacked the biometric locks on the lockers farthest from the other people in the room until he found a shipboard uniform that would fit him. Fortunately, with comms transmitting identification automatically, name stripes on the shirts were no longer required. He relocated the clean outfit to a different locker on the opposite side of the room, acquired another to shove his dirty clothes into, then stripped and showered. He would have happily stayed under the hot spray listening to the others' random chatter for hours. Instead, he limited himself to long enough to soothe the aches in his muscles and get himself truly clean for the first time since his shuttle had been shot out from beneath him.

When he finished, he donned his stolen clothes and hid his pistol at the small of his back under his shirt. The rest of the equipment could stay locked up until he returned for it or he escaped and sent a message to Stephenson to collect it.

"Gene Pryor" walked confidently through the halls toward officer country. His security level allowed Athena access to the ship's cameras, which were everywhere, and she routed him carefully to avoid crossing paths with anyone. When they did run into an unavoidable encounter, he kept his head up, pretended like he belonged, and gave junior crew members a frown and a condescending nod. Senior officers received a smile appropriate to their rank.

"Major Stephenson is waiting for you in her quarters, Jax."

Thank you, Athena. And, you know, thanks for keeping me alive and safe, too.

Her response had what he thought of as a smile in it. "Of course. As you've so often threatened, if you die, I die. Although, technically, it's entirely possible that I could live on if extracted properly."

He coughed to cover a laugh. *Even now, here, you can't resist busting my chops, huh?* She didn't reply but somehow managed to communicate a smug satisfaction through her silence. Stephenson's door slid open as he arrived.

She called, loudly enough that someone in the hall could hear it, "Pryor, finally, you took your damn time. Get in here." He obeyed, and the door swished closed behind him. She let out a loud exhalation. "Jackson, I thought I was going to have to start breaking down the doors of the Intelligence Division's secret gulags to find you. The galley sent up a couple of pots of coffee and some sandwiches. They're over in the corner. Get yourself some and sit."

His stomach growled at the thought, and he grabbed three mugs of the divine beverage and three sandwiches, then handed one of each to Stephenson as he joined her at the table. "Thanks for looking out for me. I might have twigged to the ghost, but I wouldn't have known he was after me. Speaking of which, how the hell do you know he was?"

The Major shook her head and finished chewing her

mouthful of bread, meat, and cheese. "I couldn't be sure. But Maarsen had prompted me to be on the lookout for Arlox's people, which is why I passed that word to the others. The questions he asked confirmed it, though. He was pretty good and snuck stuff about the SF captains and your team into a bunch of other innocent conversations, but he was definitely circling in toward you."

He finished off his first cup of coffee with a deep drink and thought about that information. "Okay, so they're after me. And it has to be because of Athena. There's nothing else particularly special about me."

The AI and Stephenson replied, "Agreed," at the same moment, and he suppressed a laugh. His superior officer continued, "There's no doubt he'll be on his way up here next, once he realizes you've slipped the net. Our shuttles are temporarily staying on the ship for some 'unexpected maintenance' caused by the planet's dust or some other excuse that Captain Jensen came up with, but it won't last long. He'll requisition one, and she'll have to comply."

"Throw me in a lover's coffin and fire me back to Earth?" The jump-capable escape pods, built for two, were strictly for emergency use. *The way this situation is going, it might qualify as an emergency before too long.*

Stephenson chuckled darkly. "I thought of that, too. It's too essential for the ship, so we can't give it to you. However, I do have a solution in two parts. Fair warning, both parts suck."

He snorted and almost inhaled his coffee. "Well, if *you* say something sucks, it's probably absolute hell for us mere mortals. Do tell. Wait, hold on, my cups are empty." She handed hers over, and he refilled all three, then grabbed another sandwich for each of them while he was there. He took his seat and nodded. "Okay. Hit me."

"We kill you."

Athena said, "I like this idea already."

Jax shook his head. *You, shut up.* "Care to explain that a little?"

Stephenson leaned back in her chair and sipped her coffee. "As long as you're part of the military, there will be a way to keep tabs on you. If you go AWOL, then the ghosts have an excuse to put military police on your trail, which won't help at all. So, we need to get you out of the system. But a retirement or resignation takes time to process, and that paperwork would likely get lost along the way if the Intelligence Division is paying attention. Listing you as a casualty will cut right through all that nonsense."

He nodded. "This all makes sense. I presume it doesn't involve my actual death?"

Stephenson ran her hands through her short hair. "As much as several members of your team and I might like that, no, it doesn't. It will require something much more difficult and painful than that."

She wasn't kidding about the difficult part, anyway. Jax finished sealing his backup jumpsuit.

Athena replied, "I believe Major Stephenson would say, 'Quit whining, Jackson,' if she were here."

Is there a way to turn off your ability to be a jerk?

"Sadly not, Jax. It's a feature, not a bug."

He smiled against his will. *Well, you better do your best to keep us alive, then, or that feature will be lost to the universe.* He went through the pre-action checklist automatically, verifying his suit integrity, stored oxygen levels, and connection to the *Cronus*'s systems. Everything was operating perfectly, which meant he probably needed to quit stalling and do as ordered. *You're sure that you can interface properly with a Confederacy ship?*

"I was designed by the Confederacy. I have better access to their systems than to yours."

Unless they've changed something.

"Possible, but highly unlikely for an object this small. Capital ships and military installations, almost certainly. Those are updated regularly. But in this circumstance, I think we're fine."

Easy for you to say since you won't feel the effects of suffocation if you're wrong.

"I believe Major Stephenson would say, 'Quit whining, Jackson, and get to it,' if she were here." The AI modulated her voice to sound almost like his superior officer as she repeated the comment, and it occurred to him that she could probably replicate most voices flawlessly once she'd heard them. *That might be useful sometime.*

He banged his helmet gently against the airlock's wall, which had finished its purge cycle, and muttered, "I can't believe I'm doing this. This is *so* stupid. Even for me." Then he gave the command to open the outer door, lined himself up with his objective, ran to the edge, and jumped out into space.

CHAPTER EIGHT

Whenever Jax was in space, he was struck anew by how gorgeous it all was. The closest analogy he could think of was floating in a lake at night, with nothing in your field of view but the stars above, but that didn't begin to capture it. At this moment, if not for the adrenaline raging through his veins caused by the stark terror of being out there without a ship or a tether, he might have enjoyed the experience. But probably not, given the likely chance of death.

Athena started in with her "I believe Major Stephenson" line, and he cut her off. *Focus, please. Give me a target.* He'd jumped with two pieces of specialty gear: a magnetic grapnel rifle that was currently securely attached by a cable to a hardpoint on the drop suit and a universal computer interface. Being alive to use the smaller device depended on his success with the larger one, however. A glowing yellow outline that appeared on his display showed the boundaries of the small ship he was drifting toward. A red dot pulsed where the grapnel would hit when he pulled the trigger. He drew a deep breath, adjusted slightly for his forward motion, and sent his only shot at survival flying toward his objective.

He couldn't hear the clang of contact, but when the line started to reel him in, he knew he'd hit the mark. *Okay. That's one challenge down. Thirty thousand to go. Where's the maintenance interface?*

"Ahead of the canopy on the pilot's right side."

He allowed his mind to drift while the line pulled him to the ship. His approach had delivered him to the side opposite the port, so he let a little of the cable loose without disconnecting the grapnel and climbed over to slot the proper end of the universal connection device into the opening. He'd never seen this version of the interface before although they carried separate ones for each type of vessel they expected to encounter in the field. In the thirty seconds he'd had to examine it, Jax hadn't been able to determine how it worked and stored that concern in the mental file of "Don't know, don't care." *It's not like I'm going to re-engineer the thing.*

Athena replied, "We could, probably. I would need to analyze it more fully to know for certain."

The canopy rose on its rear hinges and gave him access to the Confederacy fighter's interior. He was acquainted with fighters, as he was with all combat vehicles, but he wouldn't have been able to fly it on his own. Fortunately, Stephenson had correctly predicted that Athena had the skills to help with that. He pulled the connection device that had allowed her to talk to the ship out of its socket, detached the grapnel and threw the rifle aside since it wouldn't fit in the cockpit, then took his killing rifle off his back and stowed it in the space beside the seat. It required some careful acrobatics to lodge himself in the pilot's chair, and the experience was made all the more enjoyable by the genuine worry that he'd lose his grip and float away. *Perhaps my least favorite way to die.*

But his fears were baseless, and he strapped himself into the seat and inserted the connector into the slot in the display panel. After a moment, the ship came to life and his helmet filled with data and views from the forward and rear cameras, whose fisheye lenses showed most of the sides as well. He could throw a toggle to extend a control stick, which would probably operate the same as the ones he was used to, but he rejected the idea after a moment's reflection.

"Athena, you can handle all the interfacing, right? So I'm able to use voice commands instead of manual ones?"

"Yes, Jax. I have full control over the ship now. Shields are up, weapons are in standby, and the engine is at seventy percent." The fighter had been disabled rather than destroyed, and the UCCA had permitted the Confederacy to retrieve the pilot but not the hardware, which was more or less standard practice. *At least, enough so that they won't immediately notice that one of them is missing.* "Where would you like to go?"

That was the question. Stephenson and Maarsen had offered the Academy as an option, but if he were the hunter, that's the second place he'd look, right after the *Cronus*. Sure, the staff at the castle could and would hide him and play dumb if questioned, but that would unnecessarily put them at risk. Fortunately, he thought he had a better choice available. *A luckier one, at least.* "Let's head for Ezora."

On Jax's last visit to the scorched, arid planet, he'd arrived in a ship called the *Jigsaw*, piloted by his teammate and friend Cia Rearden, and carrying his whole Academy crew. He'd been uncertain the entire time whether that cobbled-together vessel would make it through the landing without tearing apart.

As he looked down, or from his perspective in the inverted fighter, *up* at the planet, he could at least be thankful he wouldn't have to worry about the ship breaking up on the way down. *Athena, everything set?*

"Yes, Jax. The fighter is programmed to engage the autopilot and fly into the system's sun in four minutes and twenty-three seconds."

He nodded. They were positioned more or less above the capital city, which was shrouded in darkness. The AI had judged that he could safely land a couple of miles away, on the opposite side from the spaceport. He would need to hire a vehicle when he got there, but either Stephenson or the Academy working through her had provided him with a new identity and all the associated items, including anonymous cash cards.

He gave his suit's readouts a final check, as he always did before a jump. "Okay, Athena, take us low enough for the jump, and when it's time, pop the canopy."

She didn't reply, but the ship surged forward in a large descending curve. When they reached a position similar to their previous one, but lower, the canopy exploded off its moorings and spun away. He gave it a moment to clear out of his path, then crouched on the seat and pushed himself toward the planet like a swimmer kicking off the pool wall. The familiar yellow wireframe appeared in his display, and as the atmosphere bit into his suit, he glided into the middle of it.

Jumping at night was always more enjoyable than doing so in the daylight, he'd learned by experience. Although the helmet would give him whatever level of illumination he wanted, there was something serene about floating through the darkness. It also served to hide the often-scary view of how fast the ground was rushing up to meet him. The tunnel bent to the left, and he steered into it, trusting Athena to put him in the right spot.

Her voice was a sudden surprise. "Deploying parachute in five seconds." She counted down, and at the end, he felt the familiar jerk of the metal weave chute opening and orienting him for landing. His touch down was perfect, and he gathered in the fabric and quickly stripped out of his suit. The dry, cracked ground offered nowhere to hide his gear, so he set the suit's self-destruct timer for an hour's delay, figuring that would give him sufficient time to get clear. The explosion wouldn't be huge, only large enough to consume the evidence of his arrival.

"All right. Part one down. Time to see if our luck holds."

The only piece of identifiable gear he still possessed was his comm, which he couldn't ditch until he secured a replacement. Athena used it to summon a car and take him to the *Lady's Luck* in the central area of the city of Grefta. It was three seventeen in the morning local time when he stepped out of the car in front of the casino, and it was a frenzy of activity. People entering, people leaving, people loitering out in front hawking who knew what sort of legal, illegal, or immoral products and services.

He grinned. *My kind of place.* The marquee's winking lights illuminated the faces on the street in flashes of momentary brilliance before vanishing and reappearing an instant later. The golden doors beckoned, and he passed through the one with the imprint of the kissing lips. Inside, the casino was twice as busy as the outside had been, with beings walking or stumbling in all directions and scantily clad servers weaving through them with dancers' grace.

He ran his eyes around the room, hoping he might get lucky and spot the female security guard from his team's previous visit. Unfortunately, all he saw were men and ones who seemed to tend toward muscle rather than brain, given the crowd's excessive rowdiness. *Athena, we're looking for Lady Elle. Do you have a file on her?*

"No, Jax. Do you have a last name for her?"

I don't. Keep your virtual eyes peeled for a brunette who looks like a movie star. She'll be wherever the most cash is. He stepped up onto an elevated area and peered over the mass of people, looking for a high-limit section. Of course, the true money wouldn't be on the public floor at all, but in a hidden salon, probably high up in the tall building. But the rumor was that Lady Elle worked the floor.

He spotted a pair of crimson velvet curtains framing the entrance into a side area. *Looks promising.* He dodged several drunken carousers along the way and took a circuitous path to avoid several more. By the time he was near his destination, the two guards in business suits standing to the left and right of the gap between the drapes watched his approach carefully.

He nodded at them respectfully. "I'm looking for a Lady."

The one on the right had a thick neck that continued to the top of his bald head. His face looked like someone had stepped on it and squashed it flatter than nature ever intended. The dark mustache failed to distract from his overall unpleasantness. He growled, "Maybe the Lady doesn't want to see you."

Jax shrugged. "Maybe that's for the Lady to decide."

The other guard offered, in a tone thick with condescension, "Maybe you could come back tomorrow. The Lady is probably busy right now." He was more the standard bodybuilder type and doubtless enjoyed looking at his handsome face and perfectly styled blonde hair in the mirror a little too much.

Jax flexed his hand, which suddenly itched with the desire to make him resemble his partner a little more. "Again, maybe the Lady, who has more brains in her little finger than the two of you combined have in your whole family trees, should make that decision."

Athena snorted. "Nice one."

He suppressed a smile at the unexpected compliment. *Thank you. Not sure it'll get the job done, though.*

The pair leaned forward as if they would continue the discussion with force rather than witty banter, but a seductive, throaty voice purred, "The Lady is willing to talk to the gentleman." Lady Elle stepped through the opening and bestowed a smile upon him that likely had turned many a man into her grateful servants in the past. "Captain, when I made the offer for a free tumble in the sheets, I assumed you would take me up on it with a little more alacrity." She lifted a perfectly sculpted eyebrow as she slipped her arm through his. "So, what'll it be? Blonde, brunette, or redhead?"

CHAPTER NINE

After he'd convinced Lady Elle that he wasn't there to take advantage of her hospitality in that particular fashion, she led Jax to a secluded bar in the corner. The server had a pink drink in a martini glass ready in moments and slid it in front of the casino owner with a flourish. He received a smile in return. Jax ordered a beer since he needed to keep his wits about him in the face of the woman sitting next to him. He also hoped to recover some of the moisture the planet had sucked out of his body during his brief time outside.

She slipped on her teasing tone and asked, "So, Captain Reese, if it's not one of my ladies that interests you, perhaps there's something else I can offer?" Her fingers toyed with the necklace that she undoubtedly wore to draw the eye to her tightly wrapped chest, which pushed enticingly against the strapless dress's confines.

He shook his head and laughed softly. "Lady Elle, you are amazing at what you do, but I'm here on business."

She lifted an eyebrow. "But Jackson, my business is pleasure."

"Academy business."

She dropped the flirtatious act with a sigh and slipped into the persona he'd seen during the planning session for their move against the Confederacy head-quarters on the planet. He cringed inwardly at the memory of all they'd gone through only to discover they couldn't get what they needed. *At least no one got seriously hurt or killed on either side. That's something, anyway. Well, except for the killer robot. He wasn't a friend of yours, was he, Athena?*

"No, Jax. I try to maintain a certain level of intelligence among those I call friends, and he was even less equipped than you in that regard."

Ouch.

Lady Elle observed, "One day, Captain Reese, you'll visit when you're not working for the Professor, and we'll see whether it's possible to crack that serious veneer. But for now, my resources are your resources. What can I do for you?"

His room for the night wasn't quite as nice as the one he'd occupied at the resort, but it came close. She'd pointedly not given him one of the best in the house, along with an explanation that she'd make sure he had an *amazing* experience when he visited specifically to indulge. Her flirty voice had returned for that comment. *Wonder what she sees in me?*

Athena snorted. "It's nothing personal. You're a challenge to overcome, and she likes to win."

You know, you're really not any good for my ego at all.

"Your ego is quite oversized enough as it is. Without my intervention, your skull would probably explode from the size of it."

Jax shook his head and laughed for a moment at how the person operating the camera that was almost certainly hidden in the room might react to his facial expressions as he argued with the AI. *Hey, are there video and audio pickups in here? Can you compromise them?*

"Both, and I've already done so."

Think the secure line she promised is actually secure?

"It's hard-wired, so unless you want to take it apart and connect me, I can't be sure. But I believe she is sincere in her desire to support you as long as you're working on the Academy's behalf."

He picked up the thin cable that ran into the wall and slotted it into his comm. "All right, let's give the Professor a call."

A sigh bounced around in his head as the AI did as he requested. He found her irritation at being asked to do things he could as easily have done on his own amusing. It might have been petty, but then again, she was well able to hold her own in their battle of wits.

The line connected, and a computerized voice asked, "Name?"

"Jackson Reese."

"To whom do you wish to speak?"

Dr. Juno Cray. "Professor Maarsen."

"Please stand by."

He waited for three minutes, the soft music playing in the background the only clue he was still connected to the Academy. He spent the time pacing the room, crossing from the entryway to the sitting room with its padded couch and large wall display, then into the bedroom, which held a king-size bed covered in far too many pillows. It made him want to sink into it and sleep for a week.

He was jarred from that thought by Maarsen's voice. "Jackson, we've been waiting for your call. Are you safe?"

The Professor surely knew he was calling from the casino and thus was aware he was as safe as he was likely to get. *Still, it's nice to be asked, right?* "Yes, for the moment. Thank you for the identities you sent. They will come in handy, I'm sure."

Major Anika Stephenson's voice sounded next, and it was only a small surprise. Recent events had proven that she was more deeply connected to the Academy than he'd initially realized. It made sense that she would want to speak with Maarsen in person, rather than risk someone on the *Cronus* intercepting her conversation. "No problems with the ship?"

"Got gobbled up by the local star."

The Professor laughed. "Well done. A simple, elegant solution." His voice turned serious. "So, we've been discussing your situation and have some thoughts. But first, what's your assessment?"

Jax smiled but held in the chuckle that threatened. *For Maarsen, every moment is a teaching moment.* "My official conclusion is that I'm screwed."

Stephenson's laughter rang out. "I think he's looking for

a little more on the 'what are your plans' angle, as opposed to the 'poor pitiful me' angle, Jackson."

"Oh, sorry. I thought we were honest here." He stressed "honest" to show he was joking. "All right, seriously then, we need some intel. Probably the most important thing is to figure out who's leaking information all over the place."

Maarsen observed, "And that's why you chose to go to Grefta, isn't it?"

He nodded. "You got it in one, Professor. As the center of the local Confederacy government, it has the advantage of access to lots of data, likely with less security than I'd face elsewhere."

Stephenson countered, "Except for the part where you already made a run at them there, which will have left them on a higher defensive footing."

"True. There's no way I'll be able to do what I did before. I haven't quite figured that part out yet."

Maarsen switched topics. "I have some difficult news to share, Jackson, and I might as well quit stalling. Simply put, you're on your own for a while. The only reason we were able to take this call was that it's on a line we're positive is clear. It's only ever used to communicate with Lady Elle, and I trust her ability to keep it uncompromised."

"I assumed as much. That's not an unfamiliar situation for me. No worries. What are you doing on your end?"

Stephenson replied, "Running down every lead we can find. I'm working on backtracing the ghost who showed up on Vermar. So far I've identified the ship he came in on, and we're looking for the records that detail where its previous posting was. But my guess is the Intelligence

Division has some serious talent at work covering its tracks, so the likelihood we'll find anything solid is low."

The Professor added, "I've asked several of our occasional alumni to report in with anything they know, but they haven't yet shared anything revealing." Maarsen referred to his people as "active, occasional, and passive" based on how often the Academy gave them tasks. Some of the most valuable ones, he'd explained, were in the last category. Their positions were too risky, or too important, to reach out to them; it was a one-way communication path.

Jax shrugged. "You do your best, I'll do my best, and we'll meet in the middle."

"There's an additional complication." Maarsen's voice had turned colder like he was angry. *I'm not sure I've ever seen him angry.* "The Academy and its current students are under surveillance. I presume many of our past students are as well."

Stephenson's voice carried a clearer indication of anger as she growled, "It has to be Arlox. Another move in the damn game the two of you play."

Maarsen replied, "Almost certainly. But the timing is suggestive."

Jax asked, "You mean you think he's personally behind all of this? It's not only his division doing its normal work?"

"Possible, Jackson. Definitely possible." The other man's tone was thoughtful. "But not enough information yet to be positive."

Stephenson snorted. "*I'm* positive. That bastard is at the center of this web."

"Now now, Anika. There's no way to be sure."

"I'll trust my gut on this one, Nikolai."

Jax interrupted, "So, back to the man on the run for a second. Will I be able to access the Academy's resources if I need to?"

Maarsen replied, "Maybe. We can't put out the call to let everyone know that you're seeking assistance because we can't trust the security of our normal channels. As people cycle through the Academy in person, we'll let them know. But I'm sure Elle can give you some contacts."

It was less than he'd hoped for, but pretty much what he'd expected. "Okay. How do I stay in touch?"

Stephenson sighed. "That's the other problem. You'll have to ditch your comm. I'm sure your contact there can provide a new one. But we'll have to go old school. Messages on public boards in code, that sort of thing. She should have a cipher and instructions that you can use."

Jax laughed. "So, I'm a total spy now, is that it?"

"Until we're able to bring you in from the cold, yeah, pretty much."

"Okay. Hell, it's like an adventure vacation."

Maarsen chuckled. "Except those don't usually carry the threat of death or imprisonment."

Jax grinned. "Clearly you've never seen the kind of vacationing that Special Forces soldiers get up to, Professor. This is a walk in the park."

"This won't be a walk in the park, Jackson." Lady Elle sat across from him on her white couch in her beautiful living room, with sunlight streaming through the windows and equally beautiful curtains. Jax had slept until early afternoon, had taken a decadently long shower, ordered room service, and waited for her call. His adjusted schedule was apparently in line with her regular one since that summons came soon after he'd run out of things to keep him busy.

He nodded. "I know. But I think it has the highest chance of success. What can you do to assist?"

"A new identity is no problem. Doubtless, we have several that will be appropriate. Almost certainly some tech as well. But, aside from that, the best I have to offer is transport at the ready to get you to the spaceport and maybe a diversion if you need to escape. Are you sure you don't have a better option?

He shook his head. "We broke in before, and there's no question they'll have beefed up security in this facility, and probably all their other ones as well. Doing it that way again is doomed before it begins. And that leaves only the one alternative."

"And you think you're a good enough actor to pull it off?"

Jax gave a cocky grin. "Of course."

Elle made a sound that was a mix of a soft laugh and a sigh. "You're insane. You know that?"

Athena added, "She's right."

He shook his head at both of them. "Crazy with a purpose. By tomorrow night, I'll turn this thing around, and instead of being the prey, I'll be the one doing the hunting. Count on it."

CHAPTER TEN

Jax had spent the evening before planning and coordinating with Lady Elle's people, and he felt he'd done as much as humanly possible to prepare for the day's operation. Athena agreed that she'd also made her best effort in trying to poke holes in the plan. Unfortunately, it was decidedly more punctured than he would have preferred. *But will I let that stop me? Hell no!*

The AI groaned, "You're an idiot. And you're going to get us both killed."

He laughed as he adjusted his tie in the mirror. *All will be well.*

"I should have a self-destruct mechanism installed. So I don't fall into enemy hands."

You want me to put an explosive device in my head? Under your control? Hard pass.

Athena offered, "It could be a bigger one in your torso if that would be preferable."

Jax shook his head. *No explosive implants, thanks.* He checked the time on his comm, and the absence of his military version disconcerted him. The one he wore now was high-end, as befit his cover identity, and had some special features hidden inside that might come in handy in a pinch. Still, whenever he was without *his* comm, he felt incomplete. *At least I have you, though.* The AI didn't respond. *Come on now, no need to sulk.*

"I'm not sulking," she replied primly. "I'm contemplating my demise due to your excessive stupidity and overwhelming misplaced confidence."

He laughed again. "Right. And on that note, time to go." He headed for the casino floor, where his favorite guard awaited him, looking as severe and sardonic as the last time they'd met. She led him through the doors into the backstage area, then down to the garage, kitchen, and equipment room. The vault was much the same as before. She knelt on the floor and pulled up a panel to reveal the door of a safe beneath. She punched in a code, opened it, and extracted a large box.

He joined her at one of the tables, and she set it down and hit a button on the top. It unfolded with a small *whir* of motors to display four drawers that rotated around an edge post into positions where he could see the contents of each. "Nice."

The guard nodded. "Nothing but the best for Lady Elle. Also, you realize that this plan isn't even remotely smart, right?"

Jax rolled his eyes. "Didn't we put this concern to rest yesterday?"

"I think you said, 'we'll have to agree to disagree' as you stomped off."

"Well, it's a great plan, it's going to work, and if you don't agree, we'll have to agree to disagree again."

He picked up cufflinks, each with a diamond in the middle. "What are these?"

She shook her head. "We'll be here all day if you ask questions. How about I tell you what's in there?" He nodded and pushed down his desire to annoy her by interrupting. "The cufflinks are ordinary, but can be used as glass cutters." She set them on the table and handed him a plastic case. Inside were a pair of decidedly fashionable glasses. "These interface with your comm. Scans won't register them as anything other than ordinary display glasses if you keep them in their container, but they're far more powerful than the usual variety."

Jax scooped them up and tucked them into his inner jacket pocket. "You have no idea how long I've needed a pair of these."

The guard's head bobbed as she held out two more items for his inspection. In her left hand was a class ring with a large red stone in the middle and in her right, a wide silver band that could pass as either decorative or a wedding ring. "The smaller one is a dual interface. It takes a command to activate it, and another to unlock it. One end works on Confederacy tech, the other on Alliance tech. It connects wirelessly to your comm. Until it's activated, it will appear inert to every kind of scan we know of." Jax nodded, and she looked down at the other one. "This is also undetectable until it gets the message to turn on. Then, slamming it down on any surface generates a blinding flash that should at worst stun those who see it, and at best render them unconscious for a short time. Your glasses will dim automatically."

He snatched them from her hands and slipped them on. "Amazing, although if I have to use the big one, I'm probably already toast. What else ya got?"

He wound up trading in his belt for one with a strong cord concealed inside it and accepting a pen-slash-stylus that was also a single-use stun weapon. Several other items of interest were available but didn't quite fit with the persona he was crafting. Ultimately, disguise was his best offense *and* his best defense and compromising it even in small ways was a bad idea. The pen itself was a reach since normally an assistant would carry such things for the executive he would impersonate, but he could explain that away as a gift from a special person or a good luck charm, at need.

When they finished, she escorted him to the garage and put him in an unregistered limousine that the casino used for guests who wanted to maintain a low profile. Before she closed the door on him, he offered, "Thank you for your help. Really. Please tell Lady Elle I appreciate everything."

The guard nodded. "Try to stay alive, Captain Reese, and come visit us again sometime."

"I'll do my best on both counts." Then the door slammed, and the operation was officially underway.

He strode into the vast lobby of the administration building with a slight frown. He'd found it was always better when playing a role that involved projecting authority, to set others on the defensive immediately. People *expected* their bosses to act like jerks, and they noticed it when they didn't live up to that stereotype. He stopped in the center and looked around with a scowl, then continued to the reception desk.

Only one living being was present behind the counter, and a pair of humanoid androids flanked him on either side. Jax's character, Reginald Terrigan the Third, would never lower himself to dealing with an artificial, despite his position as the chief lobbyist for a large, completely imaginary robotics corporation. He had declined to set up a meeting in advance, preferring again to leave people scrambling to accommodate him. The identity supporting his disguise would look powerful, influential, and most compellingly, lucrative to anyone involved in the technology trade for the Confederacy. *Personally* lucrative, if anyone noticed the hints of bribery sprinkled throughout the fictional persona.

He interrupted the man as he spoke over a comm. "Reginald Terrigan here to see Solomon Kier."

The receptionist blinked at him. "Pardon?"

Jax scowled. "I said, Reginald Terrigan here to see Solomon Kier. If you value your job, you'll get me an escort in the next thirty seconds." The other man blanched and babbled into his comm.

Athena observed, "Well done. You've made a worker on the bottom rung of the corporate ladder obey you."

I didn't want to, and I don't enjoy it, but remember, Reginald Terrigan is a class one bastard. And before you say it, no, it's not an easy role for me to step into.

A woman in the standard uniform of a junior executive —perfect hair, minimal makeup, tailored suit, low heels— bustled up to him. "Mr. Terrigan?" He nodded, then focused his eyes over her shoulder to suggest he was looking for someone more important. "I'm here to take you to see Mr. Kier."

He returned his gaze to her and stared at her forehead. "About time. Lead on." She attempted to start a conversation several times during the elevator trip to a middle floor, but he ignored her efforts.

Athena noted, "They are scanning us."

Makes sense. They wouldn't want to put someone as important as me through an obvious security review.

Finally, they reached Kier's office. He strode inside and smiled at the figure rising from behind the desk. "Kier. I'm Reginald Terrigan. I'm sure you know who I'm with." The man would doubtless have been researching him since the moment he'd been alerted to his presence. He offered a hand, and his host shook it. The office was pretty much corporate standard in grey and blue, and the desk's surface was spotless except for a tablet that sat in a holder to one side.

"Indeed, Mr. Terrigan. Sit, please." He waved a hand as he sat, and the door clicked closed behind them. "Coffee?"

Jax shook his head. *I would love some coffee. Damn it.* "No thanks. I only have a little time, and I wouldn't want to waste any of it. I'm here to make you an offer that will bring wealth untold to you. I mean, to the Confederacy."

The other man's thin smile suggested he'd heard that line a thousand times from lobbyists before him, and expected to hear it several thousand times more before his time with the Confederacy ended. As the person in charge of overseeing technological trade deals, he was a highly sought-after individual. It had required diverting two existing appointments, one via car malfunction and the other by a false cancellation, to create the space for Jax to meet with him. "Indeed. Do tell." He leaned back and steepled his hands.

Jax reached into his pocket and pulled out his glasses, set them carefully on his face, and fastidiously returned the case to his jacket. *Athena, do we have to get into another part of the building, or can we access what we need from here?* "As you know, I represent a company that is on the cutting edge of robotics technology. From Artificial Intelligence to pros-thetics, to the kind of androids you're using downstairs, we have innovative product lines in all of them. What we don't have is a, shall we say, 'favored company' status with the government. I'm here to change that."

Athena replied, "With a physical connection to his tablet, I can get into many systems. However, their most secure information is probably on hidden servers. I won't know if it's possible to access it until I'm deeper in the system."

Kier nodded, doubtless imagining he did so sagely. Jax thought he looked like a bobblehead. "This is the part of the conversation where I ask how you plan to justify that. We already work directly with several companies in your field. What makes yours special?"

Jax grinned, reached into his pocket, and withdrew the stylus. He held it up so the other man could see it. "This." He extended it to Kier, who leaned forward to grab it. Jax hit the trigger and a bolt of energy arced out at the man, who continued his lean down onto the desk, where Jax caught his head with his free hand to muffle the sound. *Boring conversation anyway. Athena, go ahead and unlock the ring.* He pulled it off his finger, and the silver band split in two. He found the proper end and put it in the tablet, then went around to the other side and rummaged through the desk drawers.

His glasses showed Athena's progress through the building's system, far faster than he could take in. *Find anything interesting?*

"I'm through the outer layer, and into Kier's private information and the internal network. The system has several personal nodes that have extremely powerful firewalls protecting them."

Come on. You're an amazing and awesome computer hacker, as brilliant as anyone, ever. Are you saying you can't get through them?

She gave a soft snort of annoyance. "I'm saying that they will require a physical connection. However, I have identified the individual most likely to have that information: the head of security for the sector."

Jax sighed. *Of course. He wouldn't be in the secret agent building a couple of blocks over, because the official types never get along with the secretive ones. Let me guess. He's up near the top with the other executives.*

"Three floors down from the roof."

Okay. Time to move on to Plan B.

CHAPTER ELEVEN

Plan B was rather more active than Plan A. While Athena pulled the rest of the information accessible through the tablet, Jax bound and gagged Solomon Kier with jerry-rigged items he found in the room. Finally, when she finished, he retrieved the connector ring and slipped it back on his finger, straightened his tie, and stepped through the door to the outer office. The junior executive who'd escorted him to the meeting rose from the couch and slipped her tablet into her purse. *Athena, can you access her device wirelessly now?*

"Yes, I have base access to everything now. I can't get to the secret stuff, or the security systems, however."

Naturally. He smiled at the woman. "Mr. Kier has asked not to be disturbed." Her face bent into a slight frown, and he leaned in and whispered, "He got a call. Sounded like a female voice. I think he might be busy for a while." She stopped her eye roll halfway through and shook her head.

"Very well. Allow me to escort you back to the lobby."

"After you." He gave his most disarming smile, but she

already faced away from him. *I don't think she likes her boss much.*

Athena chuckled. "Would you?"

His eyes surveyed the people they passed, looking for imminent threats, but found none. *So far, so good.* The elevator doors closed, and the car slid into downward motion before stopping abruptly. Then it started to rise. The woman frowned at the control panel and reached her right hand to activate the comm on her left. Jax intercepted it and shook his head. "I'm afraid you can't do that. Now, don't be alarmed. I'm only here for a little corporate espionage, not to hurt anyone. I will if I have to, of course, but I'm hoping you'll help me not have to. And we've compromised the elevator's camera and audio pickups, so no one's listening in."

She sighed. "I'll get fired if I do anything other than scream a lot as soon as the doors open." Unfortunately, that outcome seemed to bother her.

"You could say I threatened you." The car slid to a halt, but the doors didn't open.

The woman shook her head. "They won't care. They're scumbags, but they're also the only path to getting the job I really want, which will hopefully allow me to reduce the scumbag population over time."

Damn it. Fortunately, he'd trained to render enemies unconscious, but it was always dangerous. He didn't see another option, though. He advised, "This is going to suck, but you'll wake up in a little while. If you could maybe pretend to still be out for a minute or so, that would be great. We're actually together on the non-scumbag side of things."

She choked out a small laugh. "You definitely seemed like a scumbag on the way in."

He nodded. "A role to get inside." Without warning, he slipped behind her and put her in a sleeper hold, which closed off the blood supply to her brain and caused her to pass out. He gently lowered her to the floor in the front corner, out of sight of the parting doors. He stepped into the lobby of the lower executive level and looked around as if he belonged there while calling, "Thank you for the escort," for the benefit of the receptionist. Athena played back a recreated version of the woman's voice that sounded very close to authentic through the elevator speakers, acknowledging the comment. Then the doors closed. *Send her to the basement and put the car out of commission.*

"Already on it, Jax."

Excellent. He focused his attention on the thin man in the business suit standing behind the tall reception desk. "Reginald Terrigan to see Jason Klonis."

The man gave him a look somewhere between inappropriate condescension and very appropriate resentment, given their positions. "I don't see your name on Mr. Klonis's calendar, sir."

Jax replied with a thin smile and a glare. "That's because Solomon Kier just sent me up here. Otherwise, how would I have gotten to this floor? Surely you're not stupid enough to simply let anyone access the executive suites." He shook his head in derision. "Honestly, the lack of organization in this place is making me reconsider the government's request to work with my company."

The man sputtered, but Jax cut him off. "How about

this? You take me in to see Klonis. Then you call Kier. He might refrain from firing you for bothering him. But I can damn well guarantee you're on the street by the end of the day if I don't get to see Klonis right now." His voice dropped as he spoke, and he saw the fear overtake the other man's resentment. *Oh yeah, I'm definitely a scumbag. How's the woman?*

Athena replied, "She's conscious and yelling and banging on the doors. Fortunately, the basement is sparsely populated, and the car is mostly soundproof." He'd noticed that during the ride and concluded that the Confederacy had way too much money on their hands if they were using it to ensure elevator noise didn't bother their precious executives.

The man behind the desk swallowed and said, "Right this way, please." The entrance was similar to what he'd done in Kier's office, with Jax striding forward with his hand outstretched. Klonis, however, didn't have any advance notice, and the look of confusion on his face and the way his arm rose slowly to meet Jax's revealed his immediate suspicion. *Good quality in a head of security. Too bad it's not going to help him now.*

He maintained the facade until the door had closed behind him, then delivered a lightning-quick left cross to the man's temple to daze him, and choked him out. By the time he came out of it, still stunned from the blow, he was bound and gagged. Jax had been forced to surrender his tie to the latter effort since the office itself was downright utilitarian. Cords aplenty were stacked on shelves, with every terminating end he'd ever seen. Several tablets were scattered around, plus a couple of battlefield computers in their protective hard cases. *How stupid would it be to take one of those when we leave?*

Athena replied, "It would likely reveal your identity and suggest you are working on behalf of the UCCA."

He wiggled his fingers, and the AI released the ring so he could plug it into the man's main tablet, which was on the simple table that Klonis apparently used as a desk. The room's only other furniture was a chair for the occupant, a chair for a guest, and shelves filled with security paraphernalia. Some of it clearly there to be displayed, the rest probably items the man was working on. *Weird for an exec to be getting his hands dirty like that. Maybe he misses being a worker bee.* "I'm not sure there's any chance of that *not* happening whether we take the box or not."

"True. I'm into the secure part of the network. Oh, my, there are a lot of secret servers here."

A pounding on the door, which Jax had locked with the interior deadbolt after taking out Klonis, signaled that their time was running out. *Find what we need first. Then, whatever else you can grab is gravy.* He surveyed the items on the shelf and discovered an old-style stun pistol, probably six or seven generations back from the current state-of-the-art. He hit the power button, but nothing happened. "Damn it," he muttered and looked through the rest of the gear. Finally, he found another weapon that used a removable power cell and grabbed a spool of wire, a multitool, and a roll of tape. The knocking grew more insistent, as did the shouting of Klonis's name. Jax called, "Everything's fine here. Go away." Unsurprisingly, those on the other side of the door didn't obey. *What's the situation?*

"I've copied Klonis's server. I'm looking for any reference to artificial intelligence or pirates on the others." Windows popped into the visual field of his glasses, showing several scenes. "All the elevators are locked in the basement. Security programmers are responding, but they won't be able to break my hold for some time. One response team is two floors away in the nearest stairwell, and another is four floors away on the farthest. Someone sent a silent alarm, and everyone is sheltering in place. I expect a public alarm shortly." The receptionist and a couple of standard-uniformed security men were the ones pounding on the door. Fortunately, they didn't carry explosives or a battering ram, unlike those climbing the stairs.

Jax frowned. "Police response?"

"Negative. I have control of all communications entering and leaving the building. While I can't guarantee they won't have a wireless option on standby, all comms are locked into the common system while on site for security purposes."

He grinned and slapped one hand on the desk. "Finally, something goes our way." He looked down at the bound man on the floor, who glared at him through a mouthful of necktie. "You run a tight ship here, Klonis. I respect that." He connected the power pack to the stun pistol with a final twist and hit the activation button. The weapon came to life with a low whine. "Right on." He put the power cell horizontally against the bottom of the grip and taped it in place. A check of the enemy forces showed a squad of four coming onto his floor. *Time's up, Athena. Give me back the ring.*

After a slight delay, she replied, "Take it." Jax yanked it

from the tablet and donned it as it clicked back into a circle. He flipped the table and chair over and put them both between the bound man and the door. Quick strides carried him to the room's corner, away from the door and near the wall of windows that looked outside. He'd considered blasting them or trying to break through, but they were the same material used for transparent parts on starships. He wouldn't get through them with either of his prosthetics, or an antique stun gun. In his glasses' display, the security team put shaped charges on the door, then backed up with their rifles lifted. *Damn it. They're too smart to charge in. Bugger.*

He crouched, covered his face with his artificial arm, and plugged his ears so the blast wouldn't disorient him. The detonation turned the wooden barrier into splinters that shot upward toward the ceiling. *Nice professional work. Probably wouldn't have hurt Klonis even if I hadn't blocked him.* He rose and prepared himself for the security troops to move. They'd come in ready to cover all angles, but the fact that he could see them, and that they likely didn't *know* he could see them, gave him an advantage in timing.

The first one strode toward the door with his weapon lifted high. *Huh. They're not even going to try to end this peacefully. Bastards.*

Athena quipped, "Well, you said it yourself. Reginald Terrigan the Third is a total scumbag. I'd want to shoot him too."

Then the time for conversation ended, and the time for fighting for survival began.

CHAPTER TWELVE

Jax rushed forward and reached the door as the barrel of the gun poked through. He grabbed it with his prosthetic arm and twisted his body to the left, yanking the weapon hard enough to snap the strap that secured it to the guard. That unlucky individual stumbled inward as a result. Jax blasted the elbow of the same arm back into the man's helmet, and he went down in a heap.

Hope that didn't kill him, but I kind of lack other viable options. He made a spinning step across the doorway and fired his stun pistol point-blank at the next one in line before stopping with his back against the wall on the far side of the opening. In his display, that trooper fell backward, and the remaining two dodged his fall. One pulled out a grenade, primed it, and tossed it into the room.

Jax repeated his move in reverse, this time using his prosthetic arm and the rifle it held as a bat. He recognized the feel of Athena assisting him as his aim dipped slightly, then the stock smashed against the projectile and sent it back out of the office. Gas hissed out and quickly filled the space with a smoky mist. The troopers lifted the masks hanging around their necks up to their mouths. Those workers who had stayed to watch fled, coughing. *Thanks for the help.*

"Don't mention it. Note that the other guards are about to reach this floor."

He spared a glance and saw that she was correct, as if there had been any doubt. *Damn it. I don't want to kill these guys for doing their jobs.* But the two nearest him had to go down, and pronto. Before he'd thought it through, his body was already moving for the door again. He threw the rifle at the one on his right, and his upgraded limb gave it enough speed that the man flinched and tried to block rather than shooting. It didn't save him from being struck in the forehead by the magazine, and he fell back with a cry. Jax fired the stun pistol at the other one.

As the blast left the weapon, the gun burst apart. The plastic pieces cut into Jax's palm and left deep slices where they passed. Worse, the energy discharge numbed the limb completely. The only good news was that the last trooper was down. Jax raced for the staircase that the guards had come up and rushed inside. The door had no interior lock, and he growled at the loss of the moment he'd spent looking for one. He grabbed the spool of heavy tape he'd shoved in his pocket back in Klonis's office and pulled the end free with his teeth, then wrapped it liberally around his wounded hand and wrist, tight enough to keep most of his blood where it belonged.

His display showed the other security team on a vector toward him. *How do they—oh, the blood. Damn it.* The stairwell offered nowhere to hide, so he pounded down the steps, then skidded to a stop at the sight of yet another set of guards coming up from below. Bullets banged off the railings as he dove at the door and slammed through it. This level was a worker bee floor, with cubicles instead of offices. Heads popped up over the half-walls like inquisitive prairie dogs, and he smashed his hand into a fire alarm mounted on the wall. "Fire! Get out, go down, go go go."

They panicked and dashed for the small lanes that ran between clusters, and he used the time to survey the room. One wall was all windows, again made of something stronger than glass, although they seemed to be thinner than the ones on the floors above. Jax heard the guards shout at the workers fleeing into the stairwell he'd departed and ducked into one of the workstations. Athena still had access to all the cameras, and he watched them as they carefully entered. *Why haven't they shut them down yet?*

"They're trying. They're not good enough."

Heh. The guards spread apart. Two of them went toward the windows, and the other two moved laterally across the room. Six sections that each contained four cubicles, three long by two deep, divided the space. He fully expected that one trooper would follow the long lane that separated the first set of three from the other, and the others would walk the cross lanes. His cubicle was positioned on the second vertical lane from his foes' entry point, farthest from the window. They cleared methodically while announcing their progress, and he once again wished for less capable opponents.

He crouched and waited. As one angled to walk down his lane, Jax exploded from his lowered position in an uppercut with his left hand. It cracked it against the trooper's jaw and lifted him from his feet. He fell into the opposite workstation with a crash, and Jax turned and ran the six feet to the middle of the room. He ducked and smashed the class ring down on a cubicle wall, and his glasses dimmed an instant before the blinding light shot out.

They returned to their normal state in seconds, and he saw a guard stagger back with his hands over his eyes. The other two had gotten lucky, to judge by their rather accurate weapons fire. Jax dove and rolled to avoid it, and stayed in the middle lane hidden by the cubicles. He scurried and turned as he divided his attention between his point of view and the cameras showing his enemies. He popped up behind one as the man spun and blocked the reflexive strike from the butt of the weapon that tried to connect with his face.

Jax grabbed the gun and delivered a hard kick to the man's sternum. It knocked him off balance and blasted the wind from him through the protection of his body armor. He ducked as rounds splattered against the windows beside him, but they didn't break. *Damn it.* He charged forward and took the man down in a rushing tackle, then elbowed him in the helmet to put him out. He gave the rifle a once-over and cursed at the discovery that it had no stun capability.

He drew a deep breath, gripped the weapon like a spear, and popped up over the cubicle. The last trooper standing was pointing his weapon slightly away from Jax and traversed it with the trigger down the moment he appeared. Jax hurled the rifle at him and dropped and rolled to his left, toward the opening he'd have to take to charge the man. He came to his feet and ran forward. He saw his target duck to his right in a display window, which put him directly in line with the lane containing an onrushing Jackson Reese. He blasted into the guard, shoved him backward, and slammed him into the wall. The man fell, dazed.

Only then did he realize that the man had clipped him, and he bled from a shallow wound in his right arm. *Why do they always shoot the human arm? Damn bastards.* He reached down to his belt buckle and yanked it, then pulled a length of the cord within it free. He wrapped it around the guard twice from crotch to shoulders and knotted it. He used the line to drag the man to the windows, then pulled over the only remaining conscious trooper, the one who'd taken the blinding light hard enough to lose his vision. He patted the man. "Should come back. Now, put one hand here." He draped one of the man's arms around a pillar. "And one here." He put the roped guard's forearm in his other hand. "If you let go, you're both going to die. So don't let go."

He spooled out the rest of the line as he walked to the window. *Athena, status?*

"Guards in twenty-seven seconds or so. They've finally cleared the workers. Also, that cable probably isn't long enough."

Yeah, yeah, I know. He used the cufflinks to scrape a wide X in the bullet-riddled glass, tracing it several times to be sure. Then he stepped back, lifted one of the rifles he'd taken from the guards, and fired into his mark's exact center. It cracked under the first burst, and a large section of the middle shattered a moment later. If he'd had a few more seconds, he would have broken the sharp edges free, but voices in the corner suggested his time had run out. He yanked off his jacket and wrapped it around his right hand, grabbed the line with it, and dashed for the opening.

The icy pain as one of the pieces of transparent material sliced into his left leg was shocking enough to make him gasp, but fortunately not sufficiently distracting to cause him to release the cable. The street below with people walking on it rushed at him. *This is going to suck.* And it did. The line ran out a dozen feet above the pavement and arced him in to slam against the second-floor windows. That must have caused the guard above to lose his grip because a jerking fall of another three feet followed. Then Jax plummeted the rest of the way as the line snapped, and barely managed to get his feet under him and roll when he hit. He yanked off the belt and ran for where his getaway vehicle was parked.

Jax rounded the corner and dove into the back of the unmarked van, which turned to drive along the rear of the block toward where they'd initially broken into the building. It seemed like a lifetime before. He used the little bit of tape he had left to wrap the deepest gashes in his leg and growled the code words Lady Elle's guard had given him to redirect the vehicle from the spaceport back to the casino. It would take a roundabout route to avoid connecting the organization with him in case he was caught. As his consciousness faded, he hoped he wouldn't bleed out before he got there.

CHAPTER THIRTEEN

The voice sounded amused. "I know you're awake. We're monitoring your brainwaves. So quit goldbricking and open those pretty eyes." It was Lady Elle in her tease mode, and it was impossible not to obey. His eyelids required several tries to unstick, but he finally got them to release their death grips upon one another.

He was on his back and looking up at a white ceiling. He inwardly groaned since it was a familiar setting: a hospital, or medical facility, or medbay, or something. His body felt distant, as if his brain had been put a few feet away from it but was still connected. *Am I all here, Athena?*

"Physically, yes. Mentally, no more than usual."

With an internal sigh, he turned his head and spotted an array of medical equipment and the lovely Lady for whom the Lady's Luck casino was named. Elle was in a simple business suit, the least revealing thing he'd ever seen her wear, and stood next to the bed looking down at him. Her hair, normally exquisitely styled to be noticed, was now pulled back into a bun and secured by thin ornamental metal rods. "Okay, I'm here. Where's here?"

She gave a throaty laugh. "Again, when I invited you to visit the casino for some recreation time, this is not what I had in mind. We have a full medical facility on-site, and you're currently its sole occupant."

He nodded, and a host of aches and pains stood and shouted for attention at the movement. "Ow. What happened?"

She grinned and shook her head. "Ow is right. You jumped out a window, slammed into the side of a building, then fell and smashed yourself on the pavement—all of this after taking several impressively deep lacerations on the way out. By the time the van returned you to the casino, you were unconscious and had likely been so for a while. My medical team says that if you hadn't taped up your leg, you'd almost certainly have died from blood loss. Oh, and there's the matter of your hand, but I didn't think that's what you were asking about."

Damaging the hand, he remembered pretty well. The jump out the window was a little hazy. Athena offered, "I can replay it for you. In slow motion, if you like."

You can do that?

"Of course. I think you must have hit your head harder than expected. Better ask them to check and make sure your brain is still functional. Well, as functional as it's ever been."

Hush. Jax propped himself up on his elbows and was pleased to find only more aches, but no significant pain. "So, it seems like I owe you another one, Lady Elle."

She lifted an eyebrow and the corners of her mouth

crooked up. "Your debt is piling up, Jackson. One wonders how you intend to pay it."

"I, uh…"

She chuckled. "It's for the Academy. No remaining obligation. Now, rest up for a while, and when you feel strong enough, the Professor wants to speak to you. We have your room ready for you upstairs."

He nodded, then realized something. "Um, where are my clothes?"

Lady Elle laughed seductively as she walked away. "They were a wreck and had to be destroyed. Really, you should have seen them."

"You did?"

"Firsthand and up close."

The door clicked shut behind her, and Jax sank back into the bed. *I am so not that woman's equal. Maybe no one is other than Maarsen, for whatever reason.*

Athena replied, "You're no woman's equal, Jackson. Any evidence you might possess to the contrary is a delusion."

He closed his eyes and let sleep take him again.

Jax spent the next twenty hours under observation before he was released and sent to his hotel room, along with an escort either for security or to ensure he didn't collapse. *Probably both.* The quick heal drugs were exhausting, but he managed a brief shower before collapsing on the bed to sleep for another twelve hours. Finally, three days after his failed effort at stealth in the Confederacy administrative building, he was together enough to shower, shave, dress in something other than a t-shirt and shorts, and talk to his superiors.

He plugged in his comm and waited for the connection to establish. Again he was asked who he was contacting, and again he had to wait, but only for about a minute. Maarsen's voice sounded concerned. "Jackson, are you healing up well?"

He nodded, then remembered they couldn't see him. "Yes, mostly. The cuts were deep enough to leave some scars, despite the quick heal drugs. Not that it matters."

Stephenson rumbled, "Except that they're identifying marks. When you get back here, you should have them grafted over."

"Right on, boss."

The other two laughed. Maarsen observed, "At least your spirits are still strong. So, what have you discovered?"

Athena had passed the hours Jax was awake working to decrypt and organize the information they'd stolen from the Confederacy building. It had surprised him to learn that she couldn't operate while he was unconscious, and could only work in a limited way while he was sleeping. It had something to do with his mental state and need for rest, but she hadn't explained it in small enough words, and he'd lost it quickly after that. They'd spent an hour or so before the call talking it over since the demand for a report was guaranteed.

"Athena hasn't done all her second-level investigations yet. But it seems clear that someone working in UCCA intelligence is crossing a lot of lines, either under orders or freelance. Interestingly, the signs point to a single person connected to both the pirates and the Confederacy. I'd expected two."

The sound of Maarsen tapping his knuckles on the desk came over the line before he spoke. "That is interesting. Increases the possibility that this is off the books, of course, but also sets up that individual as the scapegoat if something goes wrong with either thing. I don't think they're likely to survive a misstep."

Stephenson added, "Anything to connect it to that bastard Arlox?"

"Nothing in this material. Basically, all we have is some mentions from multiple secret servers that all point to the same person. Athena's opinion is that the Confederacy people probably didn't know that others were also working with our mysterious intelligence agent."

Maarsen sounded surprised, which was notable. "Really? That makes it more likely that it's not a freelancer. Someone who could accomplish that, given the internal surveillance the Confederacy places on its people, has to have significant resources."

His superior officer growled, "It also increases the danger exponentially. Oh, and Jax, you'll be happy to know that you're officially dead. We received some discreet inquiries seeking confirmation, and they found what they were looking for."

He frowned. "How did my parents take it?"

"Your actual parents are on vacation at an undisclosed location, very much enjoying themselves. The stand-ins we put in their places are total wrecks."

Jax chuckled. "How good are they?"

"The best we have. The disguises will fool anyone. Only

a genetic test would reveal the deception. And we've put a visible presence around their home to prevent someone so inclined from getting near them, ostensibly to honor their desire for solitude. They do make themselves available for comm sessions, and there have been many, some with authentic reporters, some with people we're back-tracing to see if they're legit."

"Okay." That was his biggest concern with the plan to kill him off, and although Stephenson had promised it was under control, he'd still worried. *One problem to check off the list.*

Athena snarked, "Leaving only nine hundred and ninety-nine. I am *so* glad it's your head I wound up in."

Truth was, he enjoyed bantering with the AI. The problem was that since she was inside his brain, she *knew* that, so his protestations were more or less useless. *Shut it, robot.* Her equivalent of a snort of derision sounded in reply.

Maarsen remarked, "So, it's clear that your next step will need to be tracking down this agent."

"I thought I could come back to the Academy instead, maybe spend a couple of weeks relaxing and resting up for the challenges ahead. You know, that sort of thing."

Stephenson covered a laugh with a cough. "Yes, and I'm sure Dr. Cray misses you, too, Jackson. Get your hormones under control and focus on the job. What are you, twelve?"

"I totally wasn't thinking that." *I totally* was *thinking that, but I wasn't serious about doing it.* "All right, what support can you give me?"

Maarsen offered, "Elle has a set of new identities for you to use, and a line of credit to buy you passage to wherever you need to go. Since Ezora has the regional Confederacy capital, there shouldn't be a lack of transport options. Feel free to travel first class, to compensate for your delayed reunion with Dr. Cray."

The Academy leader's humor was always subtle but effective. Jax laughed. "Thanks, Professor. That won't even begin to make up for it, but I'll enjoy it anyway. And be sure to tell Juno I said that."

Stephenson asked, "Where are you headed?"

"We're still unsure. Athena is working on identifying the intelligence agents who were in the right places at the right times to have been the ones referenced in the Confederacy records. Once we know who's on that list, I guess we'll pick the nearest one and go from there."

The Professor sounded thoughtful. "I think we can improve your odds. Talk to Elle about her friend Jana."

Jax frowned, "Uh, okay. Will do."

Maarsen must have heard his frustration at being not fully informed about potential assets in his voice, and he laughed. "Jackson, as much as we value you, the Academy has secrets inside secrets. Some of those are cellular in nature. Only Elle knows who Jana is, for her protection, but I know she can probably get you access to some useful information."

Stephenson added, "You're spikier than usual, Jackson. Maybe you need to avail yourself of the R&R Lady Elle keeps offering you."

He blinked. "You know about that?"

They both laughed, and Maarsen said, "Good luck, Jackson. Once you determine a destination, have Elle connect you to a local with a secure comm. We look forward to hearing from you."

The line dropped, and Jax shook his head. "One of these days, I'm going to push back on this nonsense."

Athena laughed. "No, you're not."

He sighed. "Yeah. No, I'm not. So, I guess we need to call Lady Elle. And get some food. I'm famished."

The elegant woman sitting across the restaurant table from him gave a soft sigh. "So, he wants Jana, does he?" Lady Elle's dark wavy hair was at its most styled for the occasion, swerving perfectly to frame her face and draw attention to her eyes. Her dress enticed the gaze elsewhere, but he was careful to keep his locked on her above-the-neck portions.

Jax nodded. His closet had yielded a black suit appropriate for the venue, an expensive eatery on the fourth floor of the Lady's Luck. The décor was a bordello theme with heavy fabrics, dark colors, and male and female servers wearing somewhat less than servers ordinarily wore. The outfits left a little to the imagination—but only a little. "He believes she'll be able to do something Athena can't, I guess, although I can't imagine what that is. My passenger is highly skilled."

Athena offered, "Understatement."

Hush.

His dining companion took a slow bite before responding and somehow made the act of chewing look seductive. *She plays her role to the maximum. Admirable. Prob-*

ably tiring. In another lifetime, where he didn't have designs on a certain Earth-bound doctor, he might have enjoyed figuring out her fictional character's boundaries and discovering the real person hiding behind it. She explained, "It's not so much that she's a natural savant, although she might be since she's been at this for a long while and knows all the tricks. I do hate to bother her, though."

Jax shrugged. "If it's not doable, then it's not doable."

She offered a thin smile, and the flirting left her voice. "For Maarsen, anything is doable. But we should probably get a move on. She goes to bed early."

He checked his comm to make sure he wasn't wrong about the time, but it was indeed only seven in the evening. "Whatever you say. Lead on."

They headed up to Elle's apartment, and she disappeared into the back, leaving him in the sunken living room. He sat on the couch and waited uncomfortably. What he wanted to do was put his feet up and lie down, but the stark purity of the white fabric would allow no such thing. Outside the windows, the city's lights twinkled, and neon glowed. He made to rise as she returned, but she waved him back into his seat and sat on the couch set at a right angle to his.

Lady Elle placed a small disc on the table and commanded, "Activate. Connect to Jana." He'd expected a hologram to appear, but it was audio-only when the device responded a minute later. A voice gravelly with age called up a mental image of his grandmother when the person on the other end spoke.

"Yes, Elle darling? What can I do for you?"

"Nikolai has asked me for a favor, and now I have to ask you for one."

The other woman let out a happy laugh. "Oh, I love exchanging favors. What will you do for me in return?" The comment was so warm, and the smile on Elle's face so authentic, that he imagined the two of them would have done anything the other requested, free of charge. The exchange had the feel of a familiar ritual.

Elle made a show of thinking. "Hmmm. Well, it's not a lot of work, so certainly it can't be a huge package. How about three nights in one of the mid-roller suites, ten thousand in casino credit, and whatever meals and shows you want while you're here?"

Jana snorted in amusement. "I've never worked for so little. Five nights, twenty-five thousand, shows and meals, and a handsome escort at my disposal for said shows and meals."

His host laughed. "Okay. Done."

Clapping sounded over the connection. "Excellent. So, what do you need?"

Elle motioned to Jax, who replied, "Uh, I'm looking for an Alliance intelligence agent. I have a list of probables, but need to know who is the most likely to be engaged in a secret project that involves the Confederacy and the Coalition, sanctioned or freelance."

"Ah, I can see why you came to me. I've been watching those buggers for decades. Send me what you have, and I'll get you what you need."

Jax shook his head and handed a memory chip to Elle, who slotted it into the disc. *The Academy works in mysterious ways.*

Athena clarified, "It's only mysterious to you because your view is so narrow."

Shut up, or I'm going to start actively trying to kill you with alcohol. The AI laughed, and Jax settled in to wait for the directions to his next adventure.

.

CHAPTER FOURTEEN

While it didn't come close to compensating for his delayed reunion with Dr. Juno Cray, flying first class aboard the *Ambassador's Flight* was a definite pleasure. He disembarked feeling as well-rested and pampered as he had in a long time. The spaceport on Bledard was massive and sprawling, with separate sections for UCCA, Confederacy, and Alien ships, each of them subdivided into major cargo, minor cargo, and passenger vessels. The Sernothian system had been in the Alliance's hands for decades, and due to its location near the ever-shifting border with the Confederacy, it saw significant traffic from all three factions.

Logical place for an intelligence agent, if the person's contacts are visiting her, rather than the other way around.

Athena replied, "Indeed. Logical to the point of being obvious."

Jax shrugged. *Hiding in plain sight, maybe? Who knows? But if she isn't the person we're looking for, it's a good place to start.* He laughed internally. *Another first-class trip wouldn't be the worst thing in the universe.*

"Hedonist," Athena charged, and he laughed again.

You know it, sister. The spaceport's huge main building featured a curved roof soaring overhead and plentiful glass, plastic, and metal all around. Seating areas, bars, restaurants, and shops of every kind were scattered everywhere, all probably charging at least double the prices in the nearby city of Tasca. He found the tube leading there and bought another first-class ticket for the forty-five-minute high-velocity ride. He kept his eyes open since he was in enemy territory. If he'd been in the agent's place, he would have had a tap on the spaceport cameras with facial recognition running.

A stylish low hat in a grey tweed covered his hair, and the scruff on his face made it look as un-military as it was going to get. He wore his display glasses, but turned off, and had padding in his mouth pressed against his cheeks to break up the lines of his face. He could swallow the small pieces at need, and it required constant focus to avoid doing so accidentally. His clothes were secondhand, provided by Lady Elle, and looked as if they'd been worn daily for at least a year. They were also baggier than usual, and he'd changed his posture to convey a heavier, more stooped look. The duffel bag he'd carried on his back had added to the disguise and was now nestled at his feet as if he feared having it stolen.

Those precautions wouldn't stop a determined observer, but he hoped any surveillance system would be AI-driven and not helmed by an intelligence as powerful as Athena. "As if there are intelligences as powerful as me." *Hush.* He'd discovered that using that word produced something like irritation in his mental passenger, so he used it as often as possible.

Do you see any potential watchers?

"Three possibilities, but none appear to be focused on you. They may be transit authorities or simply overly aware passengers. That is based solely on your senses, of course. Do you want me to access the cameras and security system on this transport?"

No. Let's not risk it. For now, I'm an everyday, dirty drifter with a cool hat.

"It's not that cool."

We've been over this. It's very cool, like something out of nineteenth-century Scotland.

Athena snorted. "I believe Major Stephenson was right when she said you should control your hormones. They seem to be giving you delusions of handsomeness."

Shut it. The rest of the trip passed with only light bickering and no incidents. When they reached their destination, Jax checked into a low-priced hotel, garnering no specific attention from the man holding down the registration desk. The people in the lobby were dressed a lot like him, minus the hat. They sprawled on the couches, tuned in to their comms as if the rest of the world didn't exist. He took the stairs up the two floors to his room and grimaced at the sight of it. *We've come down in the universe, Athena.*

"You've come down. I live in your brain, which is so dusty from disuse that it's impossible to sink any lower."

Har har. Cameras? Audio pickups?

"Some of each, but nothing high end. Lie down." He did, with a grimace at the greasy feel of the comforter. "Okay, the camera will show you on the bed, and the audio pickups will get a recording of you snoring. Would you like me to send a copy to Dr. Cray so she knows what she's getting into?"

No thanks, but I really *appreciate the offer. You're too kind.* He stood and ran an electric razor over his face to clear the stubble, then swallowed the padding stuffed in his cheeks. *Ugh. I need to pack a bottle of water if I do this again.* Next, he donned a business suit, shirt, and tie from the protective plastic case inside his bag. The duffel had hidden a soft-sided leather overnight bag, and he transferred the contents he intended to keep to the new container. He stepped into comfortable dress shoes, shoved all the used clothes into the duffel, and dropped the bag into the shower stall. *Okay, let's get the hell out of here. You ready?*

"I have access to all the sensing devices in this building. No one will detect our departure."

He exited into the hallway and put out the Do Not Disturb sign. He'd rented the room for two days and was hopeful that no one would discover his vanishing act until after he'd left the planet. He took the back stairs and left the building through a security door that Athena deactivated. He walked quickly away from the hotel and kept his head down. Businesspeople and tourists filled the streets, and he fit into the crowd easily. Athena warned him of each surveillance camera and told him how to defeat them since the glasses from the last disguise were tucked inside his jacket pocket. The light streaming down through the cloudless sky had a peculiar blue tint that rendered everything a little strange. He spotted several alien species on the way, usually traveling in small packs. *I'd want the comfort of allies in an alien city too, I think.*

Finally, he arrived at his true destination, a just-below-top-tier hotel in the city's business district. The lobby was airy and well-lit, and the men and women behind the reception desk beamed as if his arrival had made their entire week. He gave his assumed name, declined to have the passkey encoded onto his comm, and received a small fob to unlock his door. He stepped out of the elevator on the forty-fourth floor and found his room. It wasn't quite as fancy as the resort had been, but was on par with the one he'd stayed in at the casino. It boasted an entryway, a mammoth bathroom with a shower built for seven, a seating area, a work area, and a bedroom with a king-size bed. He flicked on the sound system to some classical music and asked, *We good?*

Athena replied, "Yes. I'm not into the hotel's security system, but I compromised the cameras and audio pickups in the room. However, I can't speak to the security of comm connections, and you should by no means use the public tablet that came with the room for anything since it might be set up to secure biometric data."

Gotcha. He knelt before the in-room safe hidden in a dresser, punched in a ten-digit code, and the door released to reveal a small tablet inside as promised. He checked to be sure that it wasn't connecting to the wireless network, then activated it. A profile of the target appeared, and he reviewed the material. *Gretchen Paltar, UCCA intelligence, seven years of service. Not even a senior agent.*

"Better for avoiding notice."

Definitely. Has been stationed here for several years, made the tour of smaller installations before that. Her movements don't show any particular deviations. A map of the city showed a time-stamped path of her presence in it. She'd visited her workplace, her home, a bunch of restaurants, and several companies. All of it was in keeping with her cover as a mid-level government bureaucrat. *She's dating four people, apparently none of them seriously. The Professor's contacts must be into the surveillance network or something, to have this quantity and quality of information.* Pictures and profiles of her frequent contacts scrolled across the screen, and he paused long enough to take each in, knowing Athena would "remember" them if he needed them later.

Guess we go with the original plan. The timing is right. She's been out for dinner every other night for the last two weeks, so it's likely we'll have our opportunity. That leaves a few hours for a shower and a nap.

"Hedonist."

Yep.

His target had kept to her predictable schedule, which made things far easier than if she hadn't. The Professor, Stephenson, and Lady Elle had all agreed that even if Paltar were operating in a sanctioned capacity, it would be too dangerous for her to keep any evidence at her cover workplace, which appeared to be legitimate rather than an intelligence bureau in disguise.

A car had dropped him a couple of blocks away. He wore dark pants and an untucked black dress shirt and had accessorized with the tools from his operation in Grefta, which had been reloaded where needed and, in the case of the belt, replaced. As he turned the corner onto her street, he idly wondered if the class ring would go off if he primed it and punched someone.

The one-way lane that ran between the rows of opposing houses was narrow, and a continuous border of thick brown tree trunks separated it from the sidewalk on either side. Their canopies almost met above the street, and the leaves reaching in the other direction partially sheltered anyone out for a stroll from the elements. Not that any weather threatened—the beautiful night was cool but not cold, and the only thing he disliked about it was the glow of the dual moons overhead.

The houses butted up against one another, three and four stories high but only a couple of modest rooms wide. Each was made of stone or brick, with at least one window on every floor and a small staircase that led up to a fashionable door. His glasses increased the light level enough that the bright colors of the entrances and the dark shades of the different building materials were evident.

Their Academy contact's recon had revealed that the back entrances were watched over by security robots, which took them right off the list of options. Fortunately, the residents apparently didn't want the look of physical security messing with the street's serenity. So, the best choice was a fast break-in through the front entrance. He'd done it before on roads similar to this one during training sessions. Then, he'd used an electronic lockpick. This time, it would be Athena doing the opening through the near field transmissions of his comm.

"You should get a better comm with increased range. It would increase our efficiency substantially."

Focus.

"I am capable of focusing on approximately a thousand things at a time, give or take. I can't imagine what it's like to be as slow as you."

Jax shook his head. *Then why couldn't you knock out the cameras on the street?*

She didn't reply, and he made his move. He turned up Paltar's sidewalk without breaking stride, climbed her stairs, and put his comm against the sensor pad. Two seconds later, the lock clicked, and he was inside.

All right. Here's where the real danger begins.

CHAPTER FIFTEEN

"I've compromised the house security," Athena informed him a moment later. They'd expected that she would have an easy time since they were on a UCCA planet with UCCA personnel, and the Academy had many alumni working in government. They'd provided Jax with a database of master passcodes, and one of them had worked. "Recording and transmissions disabled."

He nodded. "Excellent. Okay, if I were an intelligence agent, where would I hide my most secret stuff? Any suggestions?"

"The house's systems have no records of any hidden rooms, compartments, or other secrets. Of course, they wouldn't."

He took a few steps along the hallway, sidestepping to avoid bumping into a narrow table with a bowl of decorative stones resting on top, and turned right into the living room. It was an elegant space, more formal than one would expect in a place like this. The furniture looked uncomfortable, and the paintings on the walls were utterly boring. The chamber didn't show signs of frequent use, which was a point in the agent's favor as far as he was concerned. "Eww." He spun left and walked into the dining room, which was less stuffy but still beautiful. It held a dark wood table, matching chairs with scarlet cushions, and a china cabinet of the same material. The seat nearest the opening to the kitchen was slightly askew. "So, she comes home, gets changed for a night out, maybe sits here, and has a snack. That's not helpful."

The kitchen and powder room were equally unhelpful, as were the bedrooms and bathrooms on the next floor up. On the third floor, though, things started to get interesting. Two-thirds was set up as an exercise space, with a thick target-ring board that had divots in it far larger than any dart he'd ever thrown. A kung fu dummy stood in one corner, and an inactive combat droid rested in the other. The robot appeared nowhere near as advanced as the Academy's versions, but it had two arms, two legs, a head without any features, and a heavy-looking torso.

Athena defeated the palm lock on a tall metal cabinet along the far wall, and Jax opened it to reveal an array of martial arts weapons, including a set of throwing knives that explained the deep slices. Also present were several small pistols, and a cursory inspection showed one each of stun, projectile, and energy. An empty spot suggested that she might have taken something with her to the dinner date. *Personal protection is never a bad idea. Lots of scumbags out there.*

The remaining portion of the space was a home office,

but his and Athena's fifteen-minute inspection revealed nothing. He frowned, then remembered something. "When were you going to tell me?"

The AI's voice was full of innocence. "Soon."

He shook his head in annoyance. "Where is it?"

"Directly above you." He looked up and saw the slight shadow where the access to the story above, which he recalled from the street outside, was located. A soft beep sounded, and the ladder slowly descended until the base, which had formerly seemed part of the ceiling, rested slightly above the floor. "And before you complain, we had to do our due diligence here first. Don't whine."

Jax sighed. "Never." *Times like this I'm reminded why I tend to do operations like this alone.*

Athena's tone expressed deep satisfaction. "I heard that."

"Yeah, whatever. Check for traps, please. I don't want to get my head lasered off because the real defenses are on the top floor and you're busy playing games."

He stopped climbing until she confirmed, "It's clear. Nothing other than the main security system on the next level."

"Relying on disguise. Not the smartest choice she's made."

"I'm sure she didn't anticipate coming up against a mastermind like you, Jax."

He closed his mouth. Athena scored too many points while he was distracted by the need not to get unexpectedly discovered and killed. When he reached the top and stepped off the ladder, it was into an attic room with a peaked roof running along the space's long line. Gretchen had set up a satellite transmitter near a small window covered by a shutter. Its position would allow the communication device to remain unseen from the street even when the window was open.

The opposite side of the room held six displays. Each one showed a different image. Jax couldn't identify the subjects or locations, but they were clearly drone feeds. "So, she has aerial surveillance going. See if you can figure out what she's looking for."

Athena replied, "Already on it. Also, that safe is now unlocked."

He turned to the heavy metal object sitting in the corner, then thought better of standing in front as he opened it, given how easy it had been to get into. He climbed on top and yanked the door wide, and an arrow whipped across the room and embedded itself in the opposite wall. "Holy hell." He took a quick look to ensure no other surprises waited, then descended. "A pistol crossbow. I wonder if that's what was missing from the shelf downstairs."

"Doubtful. That's most likely a permanent installation. Probably only deactivated by her comm."

"Wicked. This is less and less a house and more and more a lair. I need a lair."

Athena snorted. "You need a lobotomy. You also need to hurry. Cameras show her leaving the restaurant and hailing a car."

Several folders lay stacked in the safe, actual paper with actual writing scrawled across the surface. "Old-school. Cool." He spread them out and looked at each for a few seconds so Athena could capture them. He didn't process the information, figuring he could do that later, maybe on the tube back to the spaceport headed for another first-class ride.

The rest of the room held a backpack filled with survival supplies and not much else other than dust mites. Athena warned, "Time to go. She's three minutes out." He nodded, returned the arrow and the folders to the safe, and made his way down the ladder. He paused to be sure that it rose back into position properly. If he hadn't paid attention to that, he probably would have realized that he was under attack sooner.

The formerly inert combat robot announced its presence with a metal fist that Jax barely saw coming in enough time to partially deflect. The punch came from his right, so the blow that would have hit his temple smashed into his forearm instead and caused him to shout in pain. If he'd positioned his block any less perfectly, the bone probably would have broken. The other fist swinging in on the same trajectory meant that it was one of the spinning models that attacked in paired strikes from the same direction as the torso whirled the arms around, relying on speed rather than force to inflict damage.

Normally, though, the robots had limiters on them to prevent fatal injury. The *whoosh* of air in front of his face as Jax leaned back to avoid the second attack suggested strongly that this one didn't. "Athena, hack it." He dove and tumbled past the mechanical menace to gain the exercise space's larger fighting area, then rolled to his feet in a defensive crouch.

"Working on it."

"Work faster." He slid toward the cabinet, planning to grab the weapons it held, but the robot cut him off. It lunged forward while spinning, and Jax dodged to the right and slammed his prosthetic foot out in a quick sidekick. It rebounded without affecting his opponent, which was more or less what he'd expected. He circled away. *Had to try, anyway.* He'd hoped the robot would follow his movement, but instead, it stayed between him and the cabinet. "Damn it, Athena, this thing is kinda smart."

"Everything's smart compared to you. Apparently, opening the safe and triggering the crossbow also activated a new, more secure defense system. I'm working on cracking it, but it's not standard UCCA or Confederacy."

Jax looked around for weapons but discovered nothing but the hunk of metal rushing at him. *Okay, then.* He dipped his hand into his pocket and came out with the stun pen. Unlike a true security robot, this one had a visible seam where its "neck" descended into its torso. Combat versions kept their "brains" not in their head, but the protected center. He shifted the pen to his right hand and ran in while blocking the incoming strike with his left arm. A quick move jammed the disguised stunner into the gap between neck and torso, and he fired it. The robot jittered as the electrical blast coursed through its innards, and Jax used the time to race to the cabinet.

He grabbed the energy weapon and pulled the trigger, but the gun failed to fire. "Athena, override the biometrics." A moment later, he subdued the thing with several shots that drilled into its interior. He bent over and put his hands on his thighs. "Damn, that sucked."

The AI screamed an alarm. "Jax, down," and he threw

himself forward barely in time to avoid the energy beam that tried to take off his head. He scrambled to the side as more beams sought him, then turned to fire back, only to have the weapon shot out of his hand. The agent had returned and somehow managed to regain the house without either Athena or him noticing. *Guess the second system is more robust than expected.* Paltar's eyes showed only cold determination as she tracked the pistol at him again. *Athena, activate the class ring.* He fell suddenly, dodging another shot from her, and slammed the ruby on the floor.

Light burst from the jewelry, some sneaking through the edge of his glasses and causing his vision to blur. He rose to his feet to charge the woman and discovered that not only hadn't she been incapacitated, one of her eyes was open and tracking. *Holy hell, a prosthetic eye. I didn't know that was possible.* Jax lurched into motion and yanked the buckle from his belt as he ran for the room's rear wall. He pressed on the stud that activated the powerful magnet on the clasp and threw it at the weapons cabinet that stood beside his objective. He grabbed the line with his prosthetic hand and dove for the back window.

As he smashed through the glass—actual glass this time, thankfully—he felt the burn of a laser strike his shoulder. The injury caused him to twist involuntarily, and his side dragged across the broken edges, which sliced a shallow line along it. He let the line play out as he fell, then grabbed it at the last second and swung back toward the house to land cleanly on the tiny backyard's grass. He ripped off the belt and ran for the rear gate, only realizing as he burst through it and whipped around the corner of the brick wall that formed the yard's back boundary that he'd forgotten why he hadn't used the rear entrance in the first place.

The security robot was far sturdier than the one he'd faced upstairs, possessed far more weapons, was far faster and moved toward him with murderous intent.

CHAPTER SIXTEEN

Projectiles bounced off the pavement as Jax ran for his life, almost as lethal on the rebound as they were if they'd hit him directly. He was out of weapons unless you counted his cufflinks. They'd come in handy if something made of glass attacked him, but served little other purpose. He'd been barely aware enough to realize that no passage existed from the backyard to the front of the agent's house and assumed the same would be true for the other homes on the street.

That left him zigzagging to avoid the security robot's attacks, which now included laser blasts, and praying that he could make it to the corner before he got tagged. His shoulder screamed with the kind of pain that only burns caused, and suddenly, he was falling as a bullet deflected from the pavement and caught him in the foot. Mental time slowed as he twisted and fell, and he had the opportunity to reflect on two important facts. First, that the round had struck an artificial part of his body for once, so aside from losing his balance he was okay to continue running. Second, and more concerning, the agent was standing in the street talking into her comm and staring at him hard. *Probably taking a picture with her super eye.*

Athena sounded as irritated as he was. "Likely. You need to keep moving, Jax."

He hit the ground and continued to roll forward until he could get his legs under him. He jumped up and made it around the corner without any further injury. His damaged foot compromised his gait, which slowed him down, but he had no time to deal with it. *Athena, find me an escape route.*

"Cross the street, turn right at the next block. The city has a subway system. It won't take you to the spaceport, but it will get you to the tube station."

He turned the corner onto one of the main business streets and choked on a laugh as a wave of agony from his shoulder swept over him. *Us, remember? Can you do anything about that burn?*

Concern colored Athena's words. "I can lessen your perception of the pain, but that won't make it go away for real. It might cause you to exacerbate the injury."

He understood that perfectly. Pain was the body's warning system, and if you took it offline, it was easy to do really stupid stuff. Examples abounded of those with senses dulled by alcohol or drugs injuring themselves badly. Still, at this point, he'd take whatever edge he could get. *Do it.* He'd expected an argument, but instead received a cool wash of relief as the screaming pain reduced to a low shout. He moaned in gratitude, then saw movement from the corner of his eye that seemed out of place.

Jax had lost his glasses somewhere along the way so Athena couldn't help him pinpoint the problem. Still, when the suited figure pulled a gun from a shoulder holster hidden under his jacket, it was pretty clear that more intelligence agents were present in the city and had instructions to capture him, at least. When the bullet cracked into the stone façade of the storefront beside him, he upgraded the risk to "shoot to kill." Fortunately, stairs leading down to the subway were right ahead. He ducked, wove, and made it to them without any additional damage.

He pushed through people on the moving staircase, shoving them out of the way as gently as possible. No one fell, and he counted that a win as he burst from the bottom and curved toward the security checkpoint. He slowed to a fast walk and stopped inside a booth, fearing that the door in front of him would stay locked and be joined by the one behind him, locking him in. *Heh. Maybe the cufflinks will come in handy after all.* As the barrier swung aside, he nodded in satisfaction and limped toward the nearest car, not caring which direction it was headed. He pressed his arm against his side and felt the trickle of blood from the cut there. He slid in as the doors closed and ducked to brush off his shoes as the subway train swept out of the station.

When he stood again, they were in a darkened tunnel. Athena informed him, "About fifteen minutes until our stop, which is the third one from here. Be ready to move."

Should I switch trains?

"The timing doesn't work out unless you want to try to make it back to one of the hotel rooms in the city."

Jax very much didn't want to do that. He'd long before

learned to trust his instincts, and they told him that if he didn't get off the planet in the very near future, he wouldn't get off it at all. *Okay. This one it is. Are you into the cameras?*

"Yes. I recommend that you move one car ahead, in case they saw you while boarding."

He complied and found a position that would shield his face from those on the next platform and gave him a vantage on anyone boarding. The train stopped, some people entered while others exited, and the vehicle lurched into motion again. He hadn't spotted anyone he considered a threat stepping into his car. Hope blossomed for almost four whole seconds before Athena killed it. "There are three suspicious individuals on the train, two behind you and one in the car ahead. They are moving in your direction while checking their comms frequently."

He grimaced. *Sounds like they're looking for me, all right. I'll go forward unless you have a better idea.* No response came, so he turned and slowly shuffled toward the front of the carriage. The space between the cars was large enough that he could have stood there or jumped off, but the high-speed transit and the proximity of the rock walls argued against the likelihood of survival if he selected that option.

In the next car, he took the first available seat facing forward and watched ahead. *Where are they?*

"The one in front of you is half a car away. The ones behind, two and three cars away."

So I guess this is where it will happen. How long to the station?

"Thirty seconds."

He glanced around, searching for something he could use as a weapon. Short of breaking off the metal rail that served as a handhold for those standing, he didn't see anything. What he did spot was an emergency lever, and he rose and moved toward it. It was an old-style "break glass in case of trouble" model, so he'd have to time it perfectly. He watched and waited. The man entered as they pulled into the station, gave a thin smile as he recognized Jax, and spoke into his comm. His free hand snuck around to his lower back, probably reaching for a gun.

The train stopped, and the doors opened. A flood of people got on, separating him from the man. Athena advised, "One of the ones behind you got off the train and is watching for you to exit."

Let me know if the one outside gets back on. His next moves would be influenced by whether the man stayed behind at the station. The doors closed, and the bell that warned everyone it was about to start chimed. "He's back on the train, one car closer."

Excellent. The train rocketed forward, which pushed everyone in it toward the back. Jax smashed the glass and yanked the lever, which sent a signal to slow the vehicle as fast as possible. The standing passengers, already unbalanced, flew toward the front of the car. Jax's opponent showed his professionalism by avoiding the pile of airborne flesh but was still catching his balance when Jax's forward momentum was channeled into an elbow smash to his temple. He went down hard, and the nearby screaming intensified. Jax scooped up the agent's fallen gun and stepped through the door, then jumped off the train onto the opposing side. He raced back toward the station and hoped another train traveling in the opposite direction wasn't about to turn him into paste.

When he got there, he climbed up onto the platform and headed for the stairs. *Okay, tell me how to get to the spaceport tube.* He risked bringing the pistol out from under his coat for a second to check it and smiled at finally catching a break. *Stun gun. Means I can shoot anyone who gets in the way.* His limp had become more pronounced, suggesting more damage to his prosthetic lower leg. *Athena, can you do any diagnostics on my foot?*

"No, Jax. I am not yet that integrated."

Yet? We need to talk when this is over. He stepped onto the escalator to take him up to street level and wiped the sweat from his forehead, then cursed. *Damn it. My cool hat is back at the hotel.*

Athena sighed. "You don't own a cool hat."

The spaceport cars were smaller, unconnected to others, and didn't stop along the way. Jax sank gratefully into the only empty corner seat upon entering one. His adrenaline had long since run out, and the blood loss from his cut plus the stress from his shoulder wound had depleted his resources almost to the point of unconsciousness. *I'm going to have to start carrying stims around with me.*

"I can boost you if it's an emergency, but it will come at the cost of complete exhaustion afterward."

He laughed inwardly. *So, a literal single-shot pistol. Cool.*

"You're not making sense."

Yeah, I know. So, tell me what we've discovered to keep me awake. He shifted position and watched the car while she spoke. "The documents didn't confirm whether Paltar was engaged in a sanctioned operation, but the presence of the satellite transmitter is evidence supporting that conclusion. They did clarify the parameters of her activities. Our belief that she's connected with both the Confederacy and the Alien Coalition was correct. The tone and context of the materials suggest that neither knew she was working with the other, nor that she was an Alliance agent."

Jax mumbled, "Impressive."

"Maybe don't talk. You'll look crazy." Only one person had looked in his direction from the sound, but he didn't think he had much to fear from the elderly woman smiling at him. "But there's more here. Apparently, the Intelligence Division told her to watch out for you, specifically."

What the hell? Icy fear along his spine caused him to straighten involuntarily. *By name?*

"Name, description, and past locations. They listed your efforts to secure me and knew of your return to the *Cronus*."

He frowned. *That's not possible.*

"And yet, it happened."

You're saying that they've somehow tapped into the Academy.

She didn't sound pleased about it either. "It's the only logical explanation."

The tube slid to a halt, and Jax forced himself to his feet. *Okay, that's a worry for another day. I don't suppose you can access the cameras here?*

"Not without time, and not without a significant risk of discovery. The security here is top grade."

Then we'll do it the old-fashioned way. He straightened, ignored the hitch in his side, tried to minimize his limp, and wandered idly from the car as if he weren't a bloody, bruised and exhausted fugitive.

CHAPTER SEVENTEEN

Unfortunately, his physical mannerisms didn't fool the agents with their comm connections and their descriptions or photos of him a single bit. When he exited the train, he saw one on each end, and they spotted him. He growled, "Damn it to hell," and strode briskly toward the nearest exit. It was marked "Crew only," and he growled again, mentally this time. *Get that alarm suppressed and the door unlocked, or we're toast. For real.*

It opened as he reached it, comfortingly alarm-free, to reveal a long, dimly lit tunnel leading to a large building ahead. He saw a buzz of activity through the shaded transparent panels that made up most of the walls, as small autonomous vehicles delivered pallets of cargo to waiting ships. The smallest ones were nearest the spaceport terminal. He presumed the larger ones would be beyond the structure he was headed for. He pushed his speed up to a lope, not willing to risk another foot failure in an outright run. Occasional toolboxes dotted the route, but he didn't have time to stop and investigate. Heavy beige jackets, spotted with dust, grease, and who knew what else, hung on hooks near the door to the other building. He grabbed one and slipped it on, then stepped through the doorway.

He'd seen many warehouses on a lot of planets during his years in the military, and this one ranked right up there with the largest. It was at least four stories high with a grid network of shelves packed up to the flat roof. The cargo robots, basically giant forklifts on a mission, whirred and beeped as they sped down the lanes, flashing lights giving pedestrians an extra chance to avoid death. In other places he'd seen, the machines had kept to outer lanes for their main travel, only coming toward the middle when they were picking up or delivering in a given block. In this one, living beings were a second-order concern, a substantial distance behind maximum productivity.

Jax scampered forward along the center lane, figuring he could lose himself in the space if he got deep enough inside before his pursuers showed up. He made it three intersections up before his fear of discovery forced him to take a left and crouch in an empty spot about a standard pallet's width and depth, but about eight feet high. *Athena, what do you have?*

She sounded as annoyed as he'd ever heard her. "Nothing. Everything in this place is encoded to the nth degree. I would imagine it's on a changing key system, too."

Seems like a lot of security for a cargo building.

"A cargo building with probably millions, if not billions, in value inside it."

Fair point. I'm open to suggestions if you have any. Her silence suggested that she, too, lacked any good ideas at the moment. He peered upward, thinking that climbing to the top might give him a better hiding place. The rack offered enough handholds that he could probably make it, as long as no one discovered him mid-climb. He used his left hand to pull himself halfway up the next stack, but when he tried to reach for the lip with his right, the pain in his shoulder returned, and he let himself drop to the floor with a gasp.

Athena observed, "You've done more damage to the wound."

Yeah, I kind of figured that. He moved the arm around and discovered that the pain was manageable as long as he didn't try to reach too far in any direction. He didn't ask the AI to diminish it further, given the near certainty that he'd do something even more damaging to it if she did. *At least I can still use it, if not perfectly. A limping man is easy enough prey. I don't need to make myself a limping one-armed man.*

"Don't forget mentally challenged."

Shut it. Honestly, now is not the time. Save it for later. Contrary to his comment, her words had inspired a smile, if only for a moment.

Athena got serious again as a soft click registered at the edge of his hearing. "There might not be a later at this rate. That sounded like the door opening."

Yeah. I know. And the delay was long enough that they might have gathered reinforcements. They couldn't have that many here yet, though, right? She didn't answer, and he shrank back against the stack of cargo to his right, minimizing the possibility he would be visible from the middle lane. A minute or so later, as he was thinking of trying to make for one of the aisles that ran parallel to the center one, he heard a sound behind him. A voice murmured indistinctly, but the tone sounded excited—like maybe he'd found the person he was searching for. *Of course, they've got thermal detection or something. Damn spies.*

Jax charged out of his hiding place and ran to his left, toward the path he'd considered before being discovered. A shout from nearby generated answering calls from farther away. He narrowly missed getting run over by a forklift, and the crack of a gun sounded almost simultaneously with the clang of a bullet hitting the shelving unit right next to his head. He dodged to his right, then ran straight for the opposite side of the room, slowing only briefly before the center lane to be sure he wouldn't get run down. Yet another forklift was rolling down the next aisle, and the idea came to him in a flash. Before he could consciously consider it, he'd jumped onto the unit's boxy back end and hung on the back with his left hand as it sped toward the back of the warehouse.

More shouts indicated his foes had seen him, and he cursed under his breath. His arm was almost wrenched from its socket as the thing stopped and rotated suddenly, then headed down another line of shelves. The forks lifted, extended to grab a pallet, and withdrew it from the rack. It moved more slowly with its cargo in place, but not much. Jax muttered, "This is a really stupid idea, Jackson," but pulled himself up to the top of the vehicle and made the short climb to the top of the cargo. He was now about ten feet off the ground, and he laid flat in the hope that they wouldn't think to look up, but would assume he'd jumped off. It turned and headed down the center aisle toward the back of the building.

The plan worked, after a fashion. The forklift carried

him out the facility's enormous rear doors, which parted in time for it to pass through and clanged shut behind it. But then the vehicle turned toward a large cargo container, rather than a ship. He growled, "Oh, hell no," and retraced his steps, then jumped and rolled off the back of his ride. An abundance of spacefaring vessels, more than he'd ever seen in one place, were arranged seemingly haphazardly on the pavement outside the warehouse. He limped into a run away from where he'd last seen his pursuers. *Athena, find me a ship.*

"There are no passenger ships in this area."

His foot gave out, and he stumbled and slowed. The laser bolt that slashed through the air over his head may or may not have hit without the unintentional dodge, but the threat pushed him to increase his speed again. *I don't need a passenger ship. Anything that will get me off this planet. Hell, buy something with the Academy's accounts.*

He took a right-hand turn around another cargo container and stopped to catch his breath. *Okay, time to turn the tables.* He risked a glance around the corner and saw one enemy diverting to circle behind his position, and two more coming ahead. They were running all-out, not maintaining anything like proper team discipline. He smiled. *Finally, a break.* He instinctively timed their advance, which he hoped wouldn't slacken until they were close to the container. He pulled off one cufflink and closed it in his right fist. Then, when the moment felt right, he burst from cover and ran at the two agents.

They'd had their pistols at least halfway raised, which was an unexpected negative, but they were closer than he'd expected, which more than balanced the scales. He ducked and weaved a little without losing a significant amount of speed and sidestepped to his right to interfere with the left one's line of sight. Jax batted the nearer agent's pistol away as he fired it, and a stripe of pain along his right ear and scalp told him he hadn't dodged fast enough. He stepped in with a kick that knocked the man backward, but the other had moved out of the way, so the effort to compromise them both failed.

That's fine, I have something for you, too, buddy. Jax launched himself forward with a scream and a feint with his left hand before whipping his right up in a shallow arc, palm open and cufflink leading. He slammed the diamond into the man's skull, and the agent immediately dropped while clutching his head and curled into a ball. The other agent tackled Jax, who barely ducked his chin in time to avoid taking the blow on his throat. He twisted as he fell to protect his skull and slithered away before the man could pin him.

His assailant pulled back his left fist and brought it down in a haymaker at Jax's face. With Athena-assisted swiftness, he grabbed it in his artificial hand and squeezed. The other man paled as his bones crumbled under the pressure. Jax got a leg up and kicked him away, then got to his feet and started stumbling.

Athena ordered, "Go left, Jax," and he careened in that direction. He only realized when he looked down to see how bad his foot was that one of the others had shot him in the leg, a grazing blow that nonetheless was bleeding heavily.

He moaned. "I don't think I'm going to make it."

The voice inside his head snapped, "Yes, we are. Keep

your feet moving. Up ahead on your right is a vacuum rig. Grab it. Use both hands." He obeyed, absently noticing that he seemed to be losing sensation in his fingertips as he fumbled with them. "Now, into the container on your left."

It was one of the giant cargo containers. He wasn't sure why she thought it would be a better hiding place than getting on a ship, but his brain was closing down so he decided it would be best simply to do as she ordered. He slipped in and found a spot between two pallets that would permit him to lay down mostly under cover since pieces jutted out of them above him. Instructions involving putting on the mask and turning on the air supply were given and obeyed. His eyes glazed over, and he started to fade as she said something about slowing down his blood flow.

His last image was a manifest stuck to one of them that read "Rearden Trade Corporation."

Rearden. Why do I know that name? He was out before he remembered the answer.

CHAPTER EIGHTEEN

Waking up at all had been a surprise. Waking up in a comfortable bed, strapped down in case of a loss of gravity, was totally unexpected. A bag of water hung from the wall above him with a long tube attached. Jax drank greedily, not stopping until he'd consumed the last drop. He sighed and worked at the buckle of the restraint. *Athena, want to fill me in?*

"I saved you. You could start your extensive recitations of thanks now, that would be fine."

He snorted and slowly sat up. The world swam less than he'd expected. The surrounding room was uniformly grey and boring, including the sheets and covers on the bed that was the room's only furniture. It was about the size of a walk-in closet. *Where am I?*

"Aboard the *Siren's Scream*, a trade vessel owned and operated by the Reardens, based on Mars."

Right, I remember seeing that as I passed out. How did I get out of the cargo container?

"I used your comm to call for assistance after we took

off. They were honor-bound to help you heal, and that brings us up to the moment. We're locked in this cabin, and they might be considering contacting the authorities. I tapped into the network's entertainment level, which includes the external cameras, and the ship is still on its way to the jump point. I would expect they're waiting to talk to you before making a decision."

Great. I don't suppose there's a shower nearby.

"Not that you can get to."

Bleh. Okay. He pushed himself to his feet and swayed a little, but found his head was getting clearer by the moment. He tapped on the control panel set beside the door. "Uh, hello?"

A gruff male voice that sounded a decade or so past middle age replied, "Ah, our stowaway awakes. We had some doubts that you'd pull through."

Jax leaned his head against the wall. "I'm a little more resilient than I look."

"We counted one laser burn, one nasty cut, a bullet wound, and whatever you did to your foot. We're running a pool on what your excuse will be. I have 'thief,' and my instincts are pretty good about this stuff."

He groaned softly. "I've noticed that you haven't invited me to leave this compartment. Does the pool have something to do with that?"

"It might. You have to understand. My employers are targets for all sorts of nefarious people. From corporate espionage and intellectual property theft right on down to petty piracy. We can't have petty pirates wandering around the ship willy-nilly."

Jax laughed. "I promise you that I'm not a petty pirate."

He took a gamble based on something he'd heard in the other man's voice when he spoke about lawbreaking. "You have military in your background, don't you?"

"UCCA all the way," the man agreed.

"Well, we have that in common. I'm in the Special Forces, currently on leave. If you want to sit and chat for a while, I can give you my story. Hell, you can even put me in cuffs if that's what it takes, but I'm going to die if I don't get a shower soon. Trust me. It will benefit both of us."

The man laughed. "I think we can do without the cuffs, as long as you don't mind weapons pointed at you."

"Assuming that the people holding them are competent, I have no problem with that at all."

The door buzzed and slid open to reveal an armed guard standing outside it. The gruff voice informed him, "Shower and clothes are down the hall to your left. I'll see you in the galley when you're finished."

The shower was simple but boasted impressive pressure, and the ship's coverall was well-worn and soft, which gave him a positive impression of the person who ran the vessel. He figured that was probably the same individual he'd talked to earlier, and the man sitting at the table in the galley wore the rank insignia of a shipmaster.

Jax lowered himself into the chair opposite the likely captain of the *Siren's Scream*. His face was a little fleshy, the way that those who liked their drink on a fairly frequent basis got. He had a close-cropped grey beard and mustache, and sharp eyes that stared into Jax's. Wrinkles adorned the corners, but they looked more like marks of laughter than of anger. "Captain Jackson Reese. Let me officially thank you for saving me."

Athena gave a long-suffering sigh. "Sure, don't thank me, but thank him. Real nice."

Hush.

The other man nodded. "You're welcome, Captain. Of course, you could be lying. I'm still not convinced you're not a pirate."

"Well, at least we've gotten past the petty part. That's a start."

His host grunted, and Jax heard the laugh it inadequately covered. "How are your wounds? Care to share how you got them?"

"I suppose it wouldn't hurt to tell you. I kind of am a thief, I guess, but in service of the good guys. There's a double agent back on Bledard. I had to break into her place to get some evidence. Unfortunately, she was a little more clever than I gave her credit for. She shot me in the shoulder as I jumped out a window."

The ship's captain winced. "That sounds painful. That the cut on your side?"

He nodded. "Glass, or something like it. Glad it wasn't the heavier stuff, or I would have smashed my brains out against it." *Along with my humor-impaired passenger.*

Athena snorted. "Hush."

Touché. The other man gestured at the floor. "And the foot?"

"Security robot."

"Leg?"

"More agents at the spaceport."

The man grinned. "I think that makes you a thief. I win the pool."

Jax laughed. "Well, I'm glad I could help."

"Did you get what you needed?"

He nodded. "More or less. I wouldn't call it a resounding success, though."

"Neither would I." His host reached a hand across the table. "Shipmaster Ecklesson Tarn."

Jax shook it. "Pleased to meet you."

Tarn withdrew his hand and leaned back in his chair. "I'm afraid we're on a tight schedule. No time to drop you off between here and our destination."

"Beggars can't be choosers. Speaking of which, I'm more than willing to be part of your crew while aboard. Put me to work."

The shipmaster's smile reappeared. "That's the kind of incentive I appreciate. Lots of decks to scrub on a cargo ship."

Jax groaned. "Been a while since I had that task, but I'm sure I'll get the hang of it again right quick. How long until we arrive?"

"We'll be in jump position in about sixteen hours. Then it's another twenty from our insertion point to Mars."

"You wouldn't happen to be going to the Rearden's private port, would you?"

He frowned slightly. "Yes. How do you know about that?"

Jax grinned. "I know a guy who works there. Standring. Barrel of laughs."

Tarn scowled. "You apparently know a different Standring than I do. Prissy bastard."

He laughed. "Yeah, well, once you get to really know him you discover he's a very funny prissy bastard."

The other man shook his head. "Small world."

"Or, it could be that I unconsciously picked a Rearden ship because I had that connection. I was kind of out of it." *Or that my resident Artificial Intelligence led me to it deliberately.*

Athena replied, "Of course I did because only one of the pair of us is an idiot."

Tarn said, "Well, how about we get some food and drink into you, then put you to work?"

His time aboard the *Scream* wouldn't go down as either the best or worst of his many space transits. The captain had assigned him some tasks, but nothing harder than those given to the rest of the crew. The manual labor allowed him to limber up his muscles, which had suffered from damage and exhaustion and the cold of the cargo bay. He'd also used the time to offer Athena thanks often enough that her chill had thawed as well.

The ship didn't land at the private dome, but rather at an industrial area on a different part of the Rearden estate. Tarn must have called ahead, because as Jax waved his goodbyes to the crew and stepped down the ramp onto Martian soil, Standring was waiting for him. The man was the perfect vision of a butler, right down to the formal uniform.

"Greetings once again, Captain Reese." His face was

neutral, but Jax spotted the hint of a smile at the corners of his mouth.

"Greetings to you, Standring. Not quite how I'd expected to encounter you, I have to say."

"The experience is identical from this side." He gestured toward a small pod-like car that sat nearby. "Right this way, please."

They climbed in, and the autonomous vehicle slid smoothly into motion. It was virtually silent inside. Jax inquired, "How long to our destination?"

"The Rearden estate prison is only about five minutes away." His head snapped around to find the other man grinning openly. "Approximately fifteen minutes to the mansion."

"You're not trying to give me a super clever and subtle hint that the family is upset with me, are you? Because truth be told, I'm not so good at parsing subtlety." Athena snorted but didn't pile on.

"Master Rearden is, at worst, amused. The lady of the house is less so, but I wouldn't call her upset. The children, well, you've met them. I don't imagine your current situation will influence how they feel about you one way or the other." The last time Jax had been on Mars, he hadn't connected with anyone other than Standring and Anders Rearden, the clan's patriarch. Of course, the fact that his friend, pilot, and frequent partner in troublemaking Alicia Rearden wasn't on the best of terms with her family had probably had a lot to do with it.

"Any word from Cia?"

The other man's smile grew wider. "Master Rearden will be informing her of your arrival any minute."

Jax groaned. "Meaning they've deliberately decided to have me to themselves for a while, is what you mean."

Standring nodded. "Indeed, I would imagine you're correct."

"Awesome. Any tips?"

His traveling companion shrugged. "Be honest, be polite, be yourself."

Jax snorted. "I'm not sure that being myself will endear me to these folks."

"You might be surprised. In any case, your timing is good. You've missed the formal dinner, so I'll deliver you to the kitchen where the chef will feed you, then Master Rearden will receive you in his den."

"I'll need a map if I recall properly." They pulled up to the house, and it was every bit as big as he remembered.

"I'll escort you. Leave it all to me. You focus on impressing Cia's father."

Anders Rearden didn't rise from his chair when Jax entered the den, only waved a lazy hand from his position in front of the fireplace. His profile came into view as Jax circled to take the seat beside the other man, and he was forced to admit that whatever other benefits money provided, health and good looks seemed to be at the top of the list. Rearden's tan skin glowed with health, and he looked half his age.

The same servant as the last time bustled over with a glass of whiskey over ice on a silver tray. Jax took it and sipped. *Anders's whiskey and wine cellar are probably next on that list.* He counted himself fortunate that the head of the Rearden clan appreciated the same spirits he did.

Rearden asked, "So, have you adequately recovered from your adventure?"

Jax nodded. "Thanks to the crew of your ship. I'm sure that the Special Forces or the Academy will reimburse you for my passage and care."

The other man waved a negation. "No need. I would be a poor CEO indeed if I refused an injured person medical treatment and a ride. I got the broad strokes of your story from Master Tarn, but I sense that there's a little more to it. Are there additional details you can share?"

Jax nodded. He felt like he owed the man, and his instincts told him he didn't have to fear that the information would go any further. Of course, if Rearden found an angle he could use to promote his business, he would, which called for a little circumspection. "I was there to investigate an intelligence agent who's probably gone rogue. Her actions have overlapped into an area of concern for both the Academy and my corner of the military, so I was a natural choice to check her out. It didn't go as well as planned."

Rearden nodded. "Despite your helper?" He lifted a long finger to tap his temple.

Holy hell, how does he know about that? Jax didn't think for a second that Cia would have given out the information, even to family. He replied, "You seem to have excellent sources, Mr. Rearden."

"Please call me Anders, Jackson. And yes, we do hear things from time to time in our business."

"How much do you know?"

The other man offered a thin smile. "I asked you first."

Jax laughed. "Fair enough. I try never to negotiate with those who do it for a living. Yes, while we were more than adequate to the task of her first security system, the second didn't come online until I triggered it by opening a safe. I was clever enough to avoid the crossbow bolt trap, but not smart enough to realize it had activated another set of defenses."

Rearden laughed, sounding genuinely amused. "Ah, such an adventurous life you lead. In a way, I envy you. But I'm rather past the age where I should be diving out of windows without adequate protection. As to what knowledge I have about your implanted consciousness, it's limited to its existence and the fact that it's not UCCA in origin, or I would have known about it long before you did."

He nodded. "Those are both accurate statements, although I will offer a slight correction. Her name is Athena, and she prefers 'she' to 'it.' Rather vocally, I might add."

"So, she speaks to you? That's how the interface works?" His words were casual, but Jax caught the edge behind them and figured that somewhere the Rearden Trade Company had its fingers in a company that worked on AI.

"Yes. At length. It's almost impossible to convince her to shut up if we're honest."

Athena growled, "You'll pay for that, Jax. During your next date with Juno, if she's stupid enough to ask for one, I'm going to make you remember all the songs you hate. On a loop. Loud."

Shush. As much as I like him, he has an angle. Exaggeration is mandatory since outright lying might be caught. Rearden looked thoughtful, and his words emerged slowly. "Interesting. That would suggest some connection to your senses. Probably directly through those areas of your brain?"

Jax lifted his hands and laughed, careful not to spill a drop of his precious drink. "You're into the doctor-level stuff now, Anders. All I know is that she's there, she's verbose, and she's excellent at helping me remember things I've seen." *There, I've given him something new, but not anything that will go anywhere anytime soon.* He yawned, only partly on purpose. "I'm afraid I have to apologize. I'm a little worn out."

Anders nodded. "Of course you are. Standring will take you up to your room. Sleep well. Oh, also, Alicia should arrive early tomorrow. She's angry at someone, to judge by her voice over the comm. I'm probably the object of her anger, but I'm holding out hope it's you." His fondness for his daughter was evident in his amused tone.

Jax stood and finished his drink, then handed off the glass to the servant who suddenly materialized at his side. "Knowing Cia, I'd lay odds it's both of us."

CHAPTER NINETEEN

Jax finally made it out of his entirely spacious and decadently comfortable bedroom around noon the following day, after spending at least ninety minutes all told over multiple shower sessions. If he were the sort of person who dreamed of what heaven would be like, it would include hot showers, warm showers, and cool showers, depending on the season, with water that never ran out or changed temperature unexpectedly.

He would likely have spent another hour or so letting the spray soothe his muscles and mind if not for Cia's angry call demanding he emerge and face her wrath. He was careful not to laugh at her sputtering fury, although it hit pretty low on his danger register after all he'd been through. The mansion's staff had provided a set of comfortable casual clothes. He guessed they'd returned the *Siren's Scream* coverall and that the outfit he'd worn on his arrival aboard the ship had been burned or ejected into space.

Cia was waiting outside the door, and as soon as it

closed behind him, she dashed in and punched him in the shoulder, hard. He quashed the instinct to block, and once she'd delivered three or four more blows, she stopped and stared at him. "That's for not calling for help, you idiot. It's not required that you get yourself killed playing spy, you know."

He grinned. "It's nice to see you too, Cia. I've missed our little chats."

She punched him again, and he pretended to be wounded. "Ow, knock it off, I'm fragile. Breakable. Damaged goods."

She nodded. "I'm aware. I've been trying to convince Juno of that, but I think whatever brainwashing drugs you put in her drink must still be active. Although, you know, you might be a science project for her. I hadn't thought about that." Her anger had bled off and been replaced by her standard sarcastic combativeness, which was all to the good. "I've already seen my family today, so we can avoid them for lunch. Want to hit the kitchen?"

He nodded. "I would like nothing in the universe more."

She grinned. While he felt no romantic attachment to Cia, he was aware that she was quite attractive in her particular way. Maybe if she'd chosen to let her mother cultivate her, she would have been a classic beauty with long hair, perfect skin, and the right cosmetic surgery to make her appealing to potential partners. But part of what made her unique and interesting was that she chose instead to be unapologetically herself despite having those options. That involved a very casual approach to beauty and wardrobe.

She was dressed in what he thought of as her piloting

clothes, a pair of well-worn khaki trousers, a black tank top underneath one of the standard black button-downs that everyone in the Academy wore, and a battered and abused brown leather jacket that was as soft as satin. She led the way confidently, and Jax found himself losing track of the twists and turns as they went. *Athena, remind me to ask her if there's a map of this place we can get.*

The AI replied, "I'm not your tablet, Jax." Fortunately, her words held a hint of humor.

Right. I have the most sophisticated Artificial Intelligence that the universe has ever seen wired into my brain, but I also need to carry a tablet. Check. Cia asked, "So, are you really okay? Healed up?"

Jax nodded. "Mostly. In a few days, I'll be back to one hundred percent. Right now, I have some aches. Well, and the leg needs repairs, but that can't happen until I'm at an SF base or the Academy."

They entered the kitchen, a huge room with counters, cooking stations, and a wooden table that could seat eight off to one side. Standring had explained that the chefs and assistants ate together before each shift, as had been done in the finest restaurants for centuries. He'd also mentioned, casually as if it didn't matter, that the family had stolen the head chef away from one of the most celebrated restaurants on Earth. It was one more thing that gave the Rearden family subtle leverage over any business partners they invited to the house. Cia called, "Carlos, we're starving. Save us."

A man in a tall chef's hat waved and blew her a kiss. She laughed and sat at the far side of the table, then kicked out the chair at the end for Jax so they'd be next to each other.

"I've never had anything I disliked from him. Except asparagus. I hate asparagus. Why anyone ever created such a foul vegetable is beyond me."

Jax shook his head. "Perhaps you lack the sophistication to appreciate it."

"You're going to lack a head if you don't tell me everything right now. I'm sure that we can get Athena out of there as long as we're not concerned with keeping your brain working. I bet that's her preference, too."

Shut it, Jax thought before the AI could add her opinion to the mix. "I'll fill you in on the long part of the story on the way back to the Academy. You are planning to give me a lift, right?"

She nodded. "As soon as we get some food and can extract ourselves from my parents and siblings."

"The important piece is that we have at least one serious information leak, and maybe two. Probably two is my guess. And also that the Intelligence Division is after Athena, both the version in my head and whatever other technologies we left behind when we took her."

Cia frowned. "Evidence? I presume you have some."

"Yeah." He was interrupted as a sous chef placed a bowl of soup in front of him, and a basket of fresh rolls in the middle of the table. He reflexively leaned in to smell it, and his eyes immediately began to water. He leaned back and shook his head. "Woo. Spicy stuff."

His companion had already started eating. "Carlos does it all, but his Thai food is particularly wicked. Also, Tom Yum soup is one of my favorites. Bread will help."

He nodded and grabbed one of the rolls, and discovered it was glazed with butter and a little salt. She was right.

The soup was delicious, and the carbohydrates helped him cope with the heat factor. "First, the Confederacy had information about the *Cronus*'s whereabouts, and that I was on board. This came from a prisoner."

She interrupted, "Did you beat her up? Good cop, bad cop? Sleep deprivation? Bamboo under the fingernails?"

Jax scowled. "I broke her arm in a reasonably fair fight. Stephenson got her to talk by threatening her with the Intelligence Division."

Cia frowned. "Damn, that would make me babble until someone made me stop."

"Right? You and me both. Anyway, that's the second part. The Intelligence Division knew about me, and about Athena. Found out the first part of that before I scampered away from planet Vermar, and the second in the agent's apartment in Tasca City."

"Well, at least your adventure was worthwhile." They ate in silence until their bowls were empty. The same sous chef swept in and replaced the soup with a large plate overflowing with Pad Thai. Cia dug in immediately and sighed in pleasure. "As good as the food is at the Academy, it doesn't compare to what Carlos does."

"And yet you've voluntarily left all this behind."

She snorted. "You've met my brothers and sister. Tell me you'd want to work with them."

Jax shook his head. "No, thank you. One Rearden is all I can handle."

She snorted. "Are you saying you want to *handle* me, Jax? What will Juno think?"

"Oh, *hell* no. Wonderboy Ethan would delete every record of me ever existing, and I'd *poof* into nothingness."

She couldn't hide a smile at the mention of Ethan Kimmel, a member of his Academy team who carried a very obvious torch for the pilot.

Cia abruptly changed the subject. "So, what's your plan now?"

He'd been thinking on that question for a while and hadn't yet gotten a handle on it. "Honestly, I'm not sure. I think this is one of those moments where I need to turn to those smarter than me."

"Happy to help."

He sighed. "I was referring to Stephenson and Maarsen, actually. The little mice running around on the wheel in your head aren't really adequate to the task."

"Ouch. You are so mean. I'm going to tell Carlos not to give you any after-lunch sweets."

"I think that's cruel and unusual punishment, and probably a war crime."

She pointed her fork at him. "Last time I checked, we're not at war."

"Fair point. Now, tell me about this dessert you mentioned before I declare one."

He managed to avoid the family for the rest of the trip, aside from saying goodbye to Anders and his wife Michaela, accompanied by repeated efforts at conveying his appreciation for their help. Then it was off to the *Grace*, which was parked at the estate's private landing dome. Standring wished him well and offered, "Perhaps visit in a more conventional manner next time, Captain Reese," as a parting comment.

It felt good to slide into the copilot's seat, the first moment of true familiarity in quite a while. He sighed and strapped himself in, then remained quiet so he didn't interrupt Cia while she got them out into space and pointed them toward the third planet from the sun. Then he inquired, "How have things been on your end?"

She shrugged. "Same old, same old. A couple of extra runs, ferrying new students around on their tasks. But nothing exciting. Apparently, the Professor is reserving all the truly dangerous stuff for you. Well, and for Juno, since she's probably under orders to date you or something like that. It's the only explanation."

Athena added, "I agree. No other options are as likely."

Jax shook his head and failed to hold in his laughter. It felt like something clenched inside had released, and his mirth lasted for far longer than it should have. It made his companion laugh as well, although it may have been in pity. When he could finally speak again, he commented, "Athena agrees with you."

"Smart woman."

The voice in his head replied, "So is she."

He sighed contentedly. "You two have a real mutual admiration society going on here. Maybe we should see if we can transplant Athena into your brain."

Cia turned her attention back to her piloting as other ships came into sensor range. "No thanks. I'm still technology-free, more or less, and I'd like to keep it that way for as long as possible."

He laughed. "You could come along on one of my other

missions. We'd probably be able to take care of that particular bias real quick."

"No thanks. I'm good."

She flicked a switch and the compartment filled with sound, a classic rock mix that spanned decades. He reclined in the chair and closed his eyes, determined to enjoy every second of the interlude that fate had provided him before he had to get back to work.

CHAPTER TWENTY

"Jax, what the hell did you do to yourself?" Dr. Juno Cray's voice was professionally exasperated, as was her expression. It wasn't exactly the reunion he'd wanted, but Maarsen had insisted that the medical unit be his first stop. He'd sent Juno a brief message to let her know he was inbound but hadn't been able to do much more than that because both Cia and Athena were watching and waiting to mock him for anything he said that was even remotely flirtatious. On another occasion, sitting in front of the woman while clad only in running shorts might have been more interesting, but the presence of Maarsen and several other medical personnel kind of ruined the experience.

He shrugged. "There were complications."

She replied, "You call multiple bullets, a jagged slash from a knife or something, and a deep laser burn 'complications?'" Her straight dark hair was pulled back in a ponytail, and her minimalist makeup provided the right accents to make her look wholesome and beautiful. *Or maybe that's my opinion bleeding through.*

"Yeah, kind of. It's more or less my job, you know?"

She shook her head. "Then you might want to consider wearing armor on a more regular basis." She turned to the Professor. "I've got this. You should go. We'll need him for a while to repair the damage and to get some readings on the AI."

Maarsen nodded. "Very well. Jackson, when you've finished here, let's get together to chat. Send me a message, and we'll set it up." The other man patted him awkwardly on the shoulder and strode from the room.

Juno shook her head at the Professor's back. "He's something. Completely brilliant, but finds many of the normal rituals of everyday life less than natural." She returned her attention to Jax. "Okay, lie down on the table."

He lifted an eyebrow. "Are you propositioning me, Doc?"

She sighed, but a small smile flitted across her face. "As your doctor, I'm informing you that if you don't lie down on the table right now, I'm going to inject you with something to keep you awake for all the procedures but not allow you to move. I guarantee you will find the experience deeply frustrating."

Athena observed, "I like that idea. Let's do that." Jax quickly moved to horizontal.

Juno approved, "Very good." She gestured, and a couple of other people in white coats came over. "We'll do the leg first. Give him some broad-spectrum antibiotics, please." An injector pressed against his neck and discharged with a hiss. She lifted his left leg and ordered, "Activate restraints." Belts wrapped around him to hold him tightly in place. A support of some kind slid under his damaged limb. Above the table, four robotic arms with several articulated joints and various terminating ends spun through their diagnostic sequence. When the process was complete, two of them dipped down and gripped his leg above and below where the prosthetic portion began. A third, equipped with a medical laser on the end, moved into position above the join.

"Uh, Doc, painkillers?"

She laughed. "For a tough guy like you? You don't need any." She turned to one of her assistants. "All right, let's give him some."

Athena interjected, "I can keep you from feeling it."

Jax lifted his hand. "Wait a minute." *Really? I thought you weren't, uh, wired down that far yet.*

"I'm not. But the pain registers in your brain. I can block the signal."

Are there any risks?

Her tone was confident. "No more than with an injection, and likely less."

He coughed. *Okay.* "Doc, Athena says she can take care of it. But maybe keep some on hand, in case."

She frowned. "Are you sure?"

He gave her as much of a smile as he could manage, given that he was about to have part of his body cut off. "Yeah. I trust her."

"All right, then." She pointed at her people. "Stand ready. Athena, do your thing."

The AI told him, "Done," and he echoed the information to Juno. Then he closed his eyes because while he trusted the voice in his head, nothing in the world made him want to watch as they operated on him.

Several hours later, the procedures were done. He was the proud owner of a new, state-of-the-art prosthetic lower leg, even more advanced than his arm. It would be more resistant to bullets, which he counted as a significant improvement. Juno had mentioned during the procedure that if it had been his whole limb, they would have been able to do more. Then corrected herself and clarified that from a maximum efficiency standpoint, the best scenario would be to replace both legs at the hips.

He'd glared until she'd laughed and traded in her serious expression for a smile. "No, I'm not serious. Well, it's true that it would work. But I don't think we're at the point where you should go full android or anything."

He sat up on the table and looked down at the new leg. The metal was still visible since the skin replacement would take a few days to cover it fully. His other wounds were healed and covered with fresh skin as well, so he wouldn't have any identifying marks to give him away. *During all those times I wind up sleeping with spies and stuff, I guess. Gotta say the whole espionage thing is not like in the movies.*

"Nice work, Doc."

Juno nodded. "Hop down and test it out."

He did so and noticed her looking at his bare torso instead of his leg. "Are we checking the leg out, or are you checking *me* out?"

Juno blushed, but only a little. "You caught me. I was trying to picture how far Athena's connectors have made it so far."

He shook his head. "Ouch. Point scored, but I totally don't believe you. In fact, I think you're avoiding saying something. But I won't be distracted. Spill it, Doc."

She laughed. "Okay, you got me. Jackson Reese, will you go on a date with me?"

He grinned. "You know it. As soon as the Professor lets me off my leash."

"Well then, you'd best get dressed and go talk to him."

Maarsen handed him a drink without asking as Jax sat across from him, then instructed, "Connect to Anika." A holographic display popped up over his desk, and in less than half a minute the image of Major Stephenson appeared.

"Hello, Nikolai. What the hell, Jackson, are you trying to get yourself killed?"

He laughed, and the Professor echoed him. "Actually, Major, I was trying not to get killed if we want to be specific. Seems like that's all I've been doing for the past week or so."

Maarsen observed, "Fortunately, you seem to excel at it."

"Yeah, that. So, I'm sure you've come to the same conclusions I have, based on the data I sent. The only question in my mind is whether it's one leak or two."

Stephenson nodded. "I think it has to be two unless there's someone associated with the Academy who's also likely to be a Confederacy stooge. But I'm sure we'd already know about them if that was the case, right?"

The Professor shrugged. "You're aware of how rigorous our admission policies are, Anika. It's highly unlikely, but still within the realm of the possible."

Jax asked, "Does it hurt us to go forward as if it's two different people? As long as we avoid making assumptions based on that, we can investigate each angle separately. If they lead to the same person, well, I guess that will answer the question."

The other man tapped a finger on his chin. "That does seem like a viable approach. Do you want your team to work with you on this?"

Jax knew a test when he heard one. "No. We can't assume they aren't involved. Except for Cia. I don't see any reason to doubt her. Do either of you?" *And Juno, but I'm not going to say that out loud.*

Stephenson shook her head. "No basis to decide. Seems nice."

Maarsen stated firmly, "I trust Alicia completely. And I agree that every other student, and possibly some of the staff, could potentially be giving away information deliberately or accidentally." His frown dominated his face. "Although I knew that such a thing was almost inevitable, it still galls me that Arlox has managed it."

Jax tilted his head to the side in a question. "Are you sure it's him?"

The Professor nodded. "It has to be. No one else would have both the resources and the inclination. We've penetrated his organization, although not as extensively as I would like, and he's almost certain to have tried to do the same to us. And apparently succeeded."

Athena observed, "Maarsen may be exhibiting hyperfocus on his chosen nemesis. We should keep that in context going forward."

Good point, but probably not politic to mention it at the moment. He replied, "That makes sense. I hate the idea that it might be one of my team."

The other man added, "As I hate that it might be someone within these walls. But the only way to deal with it is to assume that it could be anyone."

Stephenson asked, "So, in practice, what does that mean?"

Maarsen closed his eyes and reclined in his chair. "First, we need to change all our codes and encryptions, but do so subtly enough that it's not apparent. I can handle that. Second, we need to have the staff dig through the current lives of everyone who works for or attends the Academy. I'll clear the first ones myself, and we'll spread out from there. Major, if you'll back me up on that, I'd appreciate it."

She nodded. "Of course. If needed, I can bring my most trusted people in, too."

Jax shook his head. "Can't assume that they're okay, either, Major. Someone ratted out the *Cronus*. This same thing will have to happen on your end."

"I know. But I have a few I trust implicitly."

"Fair enough."

The Professor continued, "Third, we need to check every one of our systems, and the castle and its grounds for surveillance devices. We already do this routinely, but it's doubtless time for a more serious search. I think we can hide that action by claiming we're cleaning for an alumni party. Of course, that means I'll have to throw an alumni party."

Jax and Stephenson laughed. She added, "You don't sound all that excited about the idea."

Maarsen shrugged. "I enjoy seeing them, but it's days of distraction with the welcomes, and the actual event, then the departures. The last one was a year and a half ago, though, so it's probably time, regardless."

"And what should I do?" Jax had some ideas about that, but he was curious about what the others thought.

Stephenson laughed. "Try not to get killed. If there's someone at the Academy who's a turncoat, they might make a move against you there. You should probably make sure you're never alone."

He narrowed his eyes and stared at the recording. *Did she make fun of me about Juno?*

Athena replied, "High probability. Apparently, she continues to picture you as a hormonal teenager."

Hush. He put on a confident grin. "I think I can arrange that."

Stephenson turned suddenly serious. "And Jackson? Be sure you have a weapon with you at all times. What's in your head is precious to the Academy, and the meat sack it's in is important to my people for some unknown reason. Don't take this lightly."

He nodded and swallowed hard. "You got it, boss."

CHAPTER TWENTY-ONE

Jax and Juno had agreed that waiting a day for him to heal up from the procedures he'd undergone would be a good idea, so he spent the afternoon kicking around the castle with no particular purpose. His goal was to keep his mind open and try to see things with new eyes, a process that Athena was more than willing to help him with.

They'd stopped off at the quartermaster for a set of display glasses, and the woman had furnished him with more than he'd expected, as usual. The unit provided more than an interface with his comm and the AI since it also had magnification options and thermal sensing. Jax gave over control to his passenger and concentrated on not crashing into things as the hallways he walked through suddenly zoomed in and out or changed colors as she scanned.

Find anything useful?

"The occasional sign of rodent activity, some spilled wine, and a couple of cracks in the floor concerning enough that I've sent a message to the castle's groundskeeper. Otherwise, nothing."

The rest of their wandering was equally productive. It did have the benefit of giving Athena a firsthand, or maybe secondhand if you were overly technical, tour of the castle. He was sure she stored the information against a later need.

He took her through the classrooms, the chamber where he'd welcomed Kenton Marshall to the Academy with a knife fight, and the exercise room where he'd first seen Cia and met Coach. The tavern wasn't open in the afternoon, unfortunately, so their wanderings finished with a quick spin through the training area and a return to his quarters to get ready.

He took a long hot shower, shaved, and put on a black suit with a white shirt and no tie. The evening ahead was a mystery because Juno refused to tell him anything about their plans. He figured that a classic dark look would be suitable no matter what. In a nod to Stephenson's advice, he slipped a small stun pistol into his inside pocket. It only held three charges but had the advantage of being no bigger than a typical business card case. Not that most people used physical cards anymore, but he could always play it off as an affectation at need.

He looked at himself in the mirror and adjusted a stray hair. "I think I'm ready. Also, Athena, if I hear any songs other than the ones I love, I'll find a way to get revenge. I don't know how, I don't know when, but it will happen. Oh, yes, it will happen." The AI didn't respond, but he sensed her amusement, nonetheless.

He worked to keep his grin from completely taking

over his face as he hurried through the castle corridors toward the front entrance. He failed at the sight of his date, who stood between the opened doors. She was sheathed in a sparkling ebony dress that showed a lot of skin from just below the collarbone up, aside from two thin straps keeping it in position. Her arms were bare, and one hand gripped a rectangular clutch in black patent leather. Her hair was up, gathered on the sides, and lifted into a pile on her head that looked structurally unsound, in his opinion. Gems winked from the combs holding it in place. Her shoes had modest heels, and what he could see of her legs was covered in dark stockings.

He stopped beside her. "Good evening Dr. Cray."

She nodded primly and replied, "And the same to you, Captain Reese. Shall we go?"

"After you."

"As it should be." She grinned and led him through the doors to the waiting sports car, a scarlet Ferrari Tributo.

His eyes tracked the car's lines in open admiration as he circled to climb into the passenger seat. The interior was black leather and smelled freshly detailed. She slid in on the opposite side and adjusted her dress as she arranged herself. "If you own this car, the Academy pays way better than I thought."

Her laugh was a little throaty and told him that she'd also been hit with the same powerful feeling of almost magnetic attraction the moment they'd seen one another. "I'd love to claim it as mine, but no. It's a rental."

"I didn't see this on the list of options at the place in Inverness."

She pressed the start button, and the engine growled to

life. "No, I've been around here for long enough to know where the true treasures lie." She stomped on the gas, and the car leapt forward. "And I have a couple of them to show you tonight."

"I can't think of anything I'd enjoy more." He mentally added, *Other than exploring your treasures. I mean, exploring treasures with you.*

Athena groaned. "You should have taken a cold shower before your date."

Go away.

She snarked, "Physically impossible, unfortunately," then faded into the background.

Juno asked, "So, let's get the work stuff out of the way. How's the leg?"

Jax shrugged. "I'd say it feels more solid than the last one, and a little heavier, but I'm sure that's my imagination. Otherwise, it's stable, dependable, and stays where it belongs. Everything a lower leg should do."

She laughed. "Very good. And you're right. It's a touch lighter." The doctor took the curves to Inverness conservatively enough to keep the Ferrari on the road, but no more than that.

"So, what's the plan for tonight?"

"None of your business. You'll find out when I'm ready for you to know."

He shivered theatrically. "Powerful women are *so* hot."

She laughed again and shook her head. "You have no idea what you've gotten yourself into, Jackson Reese."

He gave a soft snort. "That, Doctor Cray, is the literal story of my life."

They talked about random things for the rest of the

drive, catching up on their time apart. She slowed to a reasonable speed as they hit the city's edge and steered her way toward a part of it he hadn't seen. Row houses on one side with small businesses that catered to them on the other seemed to be the dominant arrangement. She pulled to the curb outside a modest tavern called the Red Door, which did indeed have a crimson entryway trimmed in black. Aside from the simple letters above it, which stretched across the entire front of the narrow building, nothing indicated what might lay inside.

She smiled as she handed off her keys to a teenager in a maroon jacket. "Don't get crazy. It's a rental, and if you break it, you'll spend the rest of your life trying to pay it off."

He nodded. "I'll treat it like it were my baby sister, Ma'am."

Juno shook her head and walked toward the door. When Jax stepped beside her, she asked, "Think we'll see the car again?"

He chuckled. "Maybe. He doesn't seem *too* wild, and you've probably put some fear into him. But I still hope you paid for the insurance."

"Of course I did. I might do something foolish and let you drive on the way back."

He grabbed the handle and pulled open the door for her, then followed her inside. The place was less than twenty feet wide, but it stretched deep along its other axis. A duo of female musicians performed on a small stage at the far end, one singing and playing guitar, the other complementing her with a banjo and a kick drum. A bar ran the length of the left-hand side, filled with what appeared to be locals, to judge by their clothing and the faces reflected in the bar's back mirror. A narrow walkway separated them from a row of small tables with chairs on one side and a black vinyl booth that ran most of the wall's length on the other.

If he'd been called upon to describe the designer's inspiration, Jax would have said "scraps." While all the decorations and furniture in the room were complementary, they were rarely identical. Wood dominated, mostly dark, and where fabrics were present, they tended toward brown, red, and black. He felt immediately at home, and more so when Juno led him down the bar to two chairs with a small "Reserved" sign on the counter in front of them. One of them held a burly man with an impressive ginger beard that reached the middle of his chest. Jax tensed, but when she tapped him on the shoulder, the man yelled, "Juno," and stood to hug her. "I kept your seat warm for ya."

She grinned. "It's good to know I can always count on you, Mac." She turned to face Jax. "I'd like to introduce you to Kieran Maclain, one of the finest doctors in Scotland."

He extended a hand. "Jax Reese." The other man shook it with a strong grip. His voice was as burly as he was, deep and growly. "So, you're the flavor of the month, are you?" Jax winced, and Maclain laughed. "I'm kidding, friend. Too often, Juno has had to while away the hours talking shop with me instead of being out on a proper date."

She slapped him. "Shut it, you, and shove off." The big man chuckled and waved goodbye as he headed for the other end of the bar. Juno slid onto the chair he'd vacated and patted the one beside her. "The people here are great. It's my favorite spot in Inverness."

He sat and ordered a local craft beer on the bartender's recommendation. Juno selected a red wine, something regional, he thought, but he lost focus for a moment while staring at her. "I can see why you like it. Spend much time here?"

She shrugged. "I try to make it down once a week, but it doesn't always work out that way." She twisted toward him, and her face went still. "So, I need to ask you a serious question. It's really hard for me, so I'd like to be sure you're not busy staring at my," she paused long enough for his brain to fill in a different but similar-sounding word, then finished, "Dress."

He set his drink down as a chill wave of concern ran through him. "Yes, okay. You have my full attention."

She nodded and seemed to marshal her reserves. Finally, she said, "I've never dated someone whose life is literally on the line as often as yours seems to be. Have you put me in your will yet?" He froze for several seconds, then burst out laughing. She joined in, then turned to the bartender. "We'll take one of everything on the appetizer menu, Bryan."

He nodded with a smile, clearly having overheard the punchline. "You got it, Doc."

Jax shook his head. "You suck, you know that?"

She lifted her drink in a toast. "Too easy. Gonna let that one pass. So, seriously though, you're doing your best not to die, right? Because I'd hate to think we have something here, only to see it ruined by your profligate adventurousness."

Athena popped in. "Those words mean 'constant danger seeking.'"

I know what they mean. You also suck. He shrugged. "Some of us do lead unreasonably eventful lives. But I promise that I'm fully committed."

"To our relationship?"

He shook his head. "To survival. Geez, arrogant much?"

Juno laughed. "Touché." Their initial appetizer arrived, baked Brie with fruit jams, walnuts, and small pieces of toast, and they dug in.

When they'd finished the first course, they followed it up with a platter of egg rolls representing different cuisines and served with a variety of appropriate dipping sauces. The last dish was an oversized bowl of lobster mac and cheese, which after a couple of drinks and given the fantastic company, Jax was ready to swear was the best he'd ever had.

He leaned back and sighed. "So, dessert? This is all on your dime today, right?"

His date laughed. "Yes on me treating, no on dessert. Can't let you get too filled up. We're only halfway done."

He frowned and offered sagely, "Huh?"

"Eloquent." She threw a stack of bills on the bar and stood. "Follow me."

Jax had no idea what to expect, which was unfortunately how he seemed to be spending more and more of his time of late. He trailed behind her as she walked to the back of the long space and turned down a staircase that opened to the right and was invisible unless you were in the rear area. It led to a room sized like the one above, but which shared little else in common with it.

The walls and ceiling were painted black, and the floor was tile that clicked under their feet as they advanced.

Cabaret-style tables and chairs, some small enough for two and others big enough to seat five or six, were arrayed seemingly at random with no clear walking path among them. Disco balls spun and threw sparkles around the space, which was generally dim except for flashing lights in every color over a central dance floor. A DJ booth rested in the far corner, and a pair of bartenders worked behind a short counter beside it. The music was high energy rock, entirely suitable for dancing, as proven by the throng bouncing in the room's center.

"Oh, uh, wow." He again displayed his wisdom.

Juno laughed, clearly delighted at the impact of her surprise. "Come on, soldier boy. There will be slow songs later. If you're good, you might get to make out with me on the dance floor."

He grinned and let her pull him forward while working hard to figure out what being "good" entailed so he could fulfill those requirements to the letter.

CHAPTER TWENTY-TWO

Jax was in the shower the next morning when his comm let out an ear-splitting alarm tone. He killed the water and grabbed a towel as a synthesized voice announced, "The Academy is under attack. All staff should report to assigned positions. All students should either take cover in their quarters or join in the defense as their skills allow. The armory is open."

He growled, "What the hell? Athena, do you have any more info?" Still damp, he climbed into one of the Academy's uniforms and slid his disguised stun pistol into his pocket.

"I've been granted access to the first layer of the security network. Drones on the outer perimeter have detected several identical cargo vans converging from the north, south, and west. Thermal readings are blocked, which the system interprets as a significant threat indicator."

"As well it should." He opened the door and saw people running in the corridors, some with purpose, and some seemingly panicked. "I assume the armory is proximate to the quartermaster?"

"Affirmative." She guided him with voice commands as he covered the distance at a fast jog, fearing that any more speed would result in a collision with a student. By and large, the halls were clearing, but several people still milled about looking confused. He shouted at them to get out of the corridors, but they more or less ignored him.

The quartermaster wasn't present, but the equipment area and the armory behind it were both open. He snatched up a pair of display glasses and an earpiece on his way to the back, then snagged a helmet and strapped it on. Sadly, it only covered the top of his head, but something was better than nothing. Next on was an armored vest that might stop a round, if he was lucky. *Wish I had my real gear.* He snagged a belt with an integrated holster and slid a laser pistol inside it, then took a rifle and two spare magazines. Getting outfitted took less than a minute, during which time three other people arrived, excitedly talking as they grabbed weapons and armor. He left the area at a jog.

"Okay, first order of business. Is Juno safe?" He would have gone to her first, but doing so unarmed would have been mostly useless.

"The security system has her tagged as moving in and out of a safe room across the hall from the medical lab." A camera image that showed a parade of white-coated people pushing equipment into the safe room appeared on his display. "It is listed as one of the highest-tier protected locations in the castle."

"Good. How about Maarsen?"

"The Professor is coordinating the defense from the operations room above the training space. It, too, is highest-tier."

"All right. Can you patch me into whatever communication system they're using?" His earpiece crackled, and professional-sounding voices reported in as they reached their positions.

Maarsen instructed, "We can't intercept the vans because we're not positive they're enemies. However, when and if we see an attack begin, the drones should take out the vehicles."

"Affirmative," confirmed a voice he recognized as the technician who had been in the booth during his last training session.

Another voice added, "Estimated arrival, thirty seconds."

The Professor ordered, "Batten the hatches." Jax jumped as metal sheets descended with loud clangs to cover the windows in the rooms to either side of him.

"Damn. Okay, Athena, patch me in to talk."

"Go."

"Reese here. I'm armed and ready to be useful, just need a direction."

Maarsen gave a small laugh. "Don't we all, Jackson. For now, the most vulnerable area is probably the main entrance. Automatic turrets cover the rear, so they're not getting in that way. That leaves several side doors, all with the same airlock system you experienced on your first trip, and the front."

"On it." Jax ran along the path Athena projected in his

display and stopped at the lobby's castle-side opening. It was a grand space with high ceilings, a stone floor, and matching stairs that curved up to a balcony above. Wrought-iron lanterns attached to the ceiling with thick chains provided the only illumination, usually meant to supplement the now-barricaded windows.

He was searching for the best vantage point when the thirty-second timer Athena had placed in the bottom corner of his visual field hit zero. Shouts sounded over the comm a few seconds before the front doors blasted off their hinges in a huge explosion. He dove out of the way of the debris that flew into the hallway, then reviewed the cameras that appeared on his display. They were clearly drone footage and showed three matching vans in addition to what looked like it had once been a sedan, but was now only burning wreckage in the doorway. *Clever. We focused on the vans and didn't spot the car.* The cameras swooped lower and lower, showing combat-suited people with rifles piling out of the vans. Their feeds vanished with the echoing crash of a trio of explosions that he heard through his comm and outside the walls.

He crabbed across the walkway and crouched behind the two-foot wall that separated the lobby from the hallway's left and right edges. He leaned out enough to train his rifle on the entrance. Athena put the lobby cameras into his display, and he tuned back into the conversation on the comm.

Maarsen reported, "Drones show that we have three independent teams outside, six in each. They're in full military battle armor." Jax cursed mentally. The heavy gear traded off speed for protection, and his pistols would be useless against it. His rifle would fare better, but he'd still have to ensure that he aimed his shots where they might hit a spot between ballistic plates.

The Professor continued, "All non-combatants should head to the nearest safe space." His comm lit up with a map that Athena quickly killed. "All staff should coalesce into fire teams of at least three members. Be aware that all interior defenses are now active. Your transponders will keep you from setting them off, but they *will* activate if you're in proximity to an intruder."

Wow, pretty brutal. Maarsen's not playing games.

Athena replied, "They're nonlethal, but your point is still valid."

"Yeah it is," he muttered. *Make sure you highlight those for me if we wind up moving, please.*

"Will do."

An enemy stepped around the flaming wreckage, supported by another who moved up next to the first. Jax knew they'd be using thermal detection in their full helmet displays, on which he'd stand out as an obvious target. He pulled the trigger the instant he had a shot, aiming for the upper chest, neck, and head. He held it down until the magazine clicked empty and had the pleasure of watching his foe stagger backward and fall onto the still-burning car.

The other hosed down his position indiscriminately, but the bullets didn't make it through the thick stone. The grenade that the armored figure launched from the gun's second barrel had a much better chance. Jax reacted by reflex as he turned and ran away. The explosion blew out a chunk of the wall, but he'd gained enough distance that the fragment didn't reach him, only clattered on the floor behind him.

He activated his microphone. "They have grenades, and apparently no compunction about killing."

Maarsen's voice came into his ear. "Jackson, we're on a private channel. We've identified the technology. These are UCCA troops. It's probable the Intelligence Division is behind it, and that you're the object of this attack. Under no circumstances can you allow yourself to be captured or killed. You should make your way toward the medical lab safe room immediately."

Jax cursed, turned a corner, and increased his speed again. "Which means that they're not our enemies and we shouldn't kill them. Damn it, that's not cool."

"The castle has a sufficient number of traps to blunt their assault, I believe. The Academy's staff will attempt to remain nonlethal, but they're under orders to protect themselves first, the students second, and only after that to give any thought to the enemy's well-being."

"Just how I'd do it, Professor. I'll try to get to a safe room." He killed his mic and turned toward a back room he'd noticed during one of his many wanders through the building.

Athena observed, "You're not planning to go to the safe room, are you?"

Eventually.

"Do you think the Professor believed you were on your way?"

Doubtful. Jax laughed inwardly. *Turns out, I tell a lot of lies in my line of work.* He pushed open the door into the small museum that celebrated the castle's past. His rifle went carefully into a corner since he felt safe leaving the empty weapon behind. He found a pair of knives, each about the length of his forearms, and a belt to hold them. Then he grabbed a pistol crossbow, two bracers each containing five short bolts, and finally a wicked spiked mace with a leather thong that also went around his wrist. *The armor isn't as good against edged weapons, since we don't face them often. These ought to prove effective, though. Now we can head toward the safe room. But if you see any threats along the way, vector me in their direction. We have some smashing to do.*

"Why not simply leave it to the castle's defenses?"

Two reasons. Jax stuck his head out the door, made sure the coast was clear and headed toward the wing that contained the medical area. *First, I know how those suits work. Stun won't be effective against them. Neither will gas. Unless we're talking about pits and trap doors, whatever defenses they've got aren't likely to be all that useful, assuming the other side has any competence at all. And I think we have to assume they do.*

The AI sounded thoughtful. "Makes sense. You might be able to crack helmets with the crossbow. Then the gas would work."

As long as I'm not where the gas is, it's an excellent plan. The second reason, though, is the more important one. I'll hide if that increases everyone else's safety, but if they're looking for me, that's exactly what they'll expect me to do. Given that they know I'm here, right now, there has to be a mole who's been present during the last couple of days or was informed of my arrival. They couldn't have put this together based on spotting me last night. It's too well-coordinated. So, the likelihood that we'll have enemies waiting for us along that path is pretty darn good.

Suddenly, the camera feeds in his display winked out all at once. *Athena?*

"The security system's down. So are comms. I have no surveillance."

So be it. He hefted the mace and swung it once for practice. *It's smashing time.*

CHAPTER TWENTY-THREE

It had been a while since Jax had been so entirely on his own. He realized as he ghosted through the corridors, trying his best to be quiet and listen for any enemy, how much he'd come to rely on various technologies. *Especially Athena.*

Her droll voice replied, "You're too kind."

Unfortunately, it's true. Now that I don't have those advantages, I miss them. He heard the scuff of a foot from the right edge of the intersection ahead and put his back to the wall on that side. He let the mace dangle while he primed the crossbow and positioned a bolt. *What should I try first, the helmet or the armor?*

"Based on the information I stored earlier, we passed a knockout gas trap halfway down this corridor. If you were to crack his helmet and run away, he might follow and fall to the trap."

He might also shoot me in the back while I go. No, I think I'll try the armor. Going for a leg. That was his plan in all circumstances, except for trying to compromise a helmet.

He could break legs and knees and hopefully immobilize the attackers without killing them. Then the Professor's people could mop them up and turn them over to the police, who would doubtless be completely unsurprised when a government official stepped in to take charge of them.

The enemy soldier's rifle barrel appeared first, followed by his lead leg. Jax led his movement and pulled the trigger. The weapon made a loud snapping sound as the taut string sent the bolt flying at his foe. It smacked solidly into the outside of his thigh. The figure grabbed it with a shout muffled by the full helmet and fell to the floor. Jax leapt forward and stomped on the gun barrel, then whipped his mace up at the second enemy who had stepped into view around the corner.

The spiked head of the weapon smashed into his foe's rifle, knocked it upward, and sent a line of bullets into the stonework of the wall and ceiling. He stepped in with a quick sidekick to the knee, but the enemy soldier protected the joint by dropping so the strike caught the thigh. It also had the added effect of taking away the targets Jax was aiming for, leaving him no choice but to slam the mace into the figure's upper arm instead. The spikes penetrated, and blood spurted from the wound as he yanked the weapon free. Jax dropped his crossbow, grabbed his opponent's helmet, and gave it a twist and a yank to pull it off. A pale face covered in sweat looked up at him. He let go of the crossbow and punched the man in the center of his forehead, right above his nose. His opponent fell to the floor, dazed.

Jax knelt and fumbled at the man's equipment belt, and

quickly found a familiar med-pack. He slapped a bandage on the wound in his arm and injected him with enough painkiller to keep him happily immobile for at least half an hour. The process was a little slower on the first one he'd knocked down due to needing to tear the bandage to leave the bolt in place in case it had punctured a major blood vessel.

He picked up the crossbow and reloaded. *Two down, way too many to go*. He continued forward on the route Athena provided to the safe room across from the medical lab. It wasn't the most direct line, he noted as he painstakingly crept down a spiral staircase to the basement, but he trusted her to run the probabilities and take him along a path where he'd encounter the least opposition.

However, "least" didn't equate to "none." Despite his best efforts to scan for thermal emissions, his enemies' suits were adequate to hide them down here in the chill lower level. A scrape of a boot was all that warned him of their presence, and he leapt to the side an instant ahead of the stun bolt that would have taken him out of the fight. *Should have had that on wide beam, given my lack of armor. These people are above average, but they're not top of the barrel.*

He dove and rolled to avoid the blast from the second attacker, and cursed under his breath as the mace scraped on the stone floor and gave a hint to his location. *But they have displays too, so their vision is as good or better than mine in this darkness.* He fired the crossbow at the nearest enemy, and it struck a glancing blow on his thigh. He kept moving, trying to position himself so that an errant shot would catch one of his foes. They were willing to wait as they maneuvered to keep him between them but didn't fire. *Of course, they're calling for backup. Damn it to hell.*

Athena, what can you do to help? A stun blast cracked past his head, only missing because he'd changed direction suddenly. He feinted at the nearest opponent, which caused him to step back into a defensive stance, then charged at the second. He tossed the mace from his left hand to his right and whipped it down at his foe's knee. The soldier lifted the joint to his chest and tried to stomp on the weapon. Jax let him, then pistoned a punch into the man's sternum with his prosthetic arm. Despite the armor there, the blow knocked him backward, and from the way he curled up for an instant, probably took his breath away as well.

But Jax had no opportunity to follow up. The sound of the second one switching his pistol into a different mode alerted him, and he dropped to the floor with a yelp. A broad beam stun blast crackled past him and caught the other, but his armor quickly absorbed it. *Right, they're stun-proof. I have to get my head in the game here.*

Athena announced, "I've got you," and muffled cries came from both opponents. They simultaneously reached up and ripped off their helmets and threw them aside. Jax moved before they'd finished. He drew his pocket stun gun, jammed it against the uninjured one's neck, and pressed the firing stud. The man fell. The other soldier was a woman, and she was still trying to return to proper breathing. She tried to shoot him, but the blast went awry as he ducked and dodged. Then she was out too.

"Damn, Athena, good work. What did you do?"

"I've been working on cracking into their systems. The

comms turned out to be most vulnerable, so I put a feed-back loop in it, increased the volume, and locked out any other changes."

"Nice. Took out these two effectively."

The AI sounded smug. "Actually, assuming no variables I'm unaware of, it should have affected all the attackers."

Jax chuckled. "Even better." He picked up both stun pistols since helmetless opponents were vulnerable. One went into the back of his belt, and the other stayed in his hand. He looked down at the crossbow with a reluctant frown, stripped off the cuffs with the remaining bolts, and dropped them with the historic ranged weapon. He grabbed the mace and turned back the way he'd come.

"Jax, you're no longer heading toward the safe room. Did you hit your head?"

"Nope. Circumstances have changed. If they're helmet-less, they can be stunned. And that's something I'm prob-ably much better at than the rest of the castle staff. Keep trying to get me some cameras, will you?"

"Unlike you, I can multitask without losing effective-ness. I've been doing so since they went down."

He reached the top of the spiral staircase and crouched to listen. *Not doing a great job of it apparently, oh supreme multi-tasker.* He heard a noise from his right and peered around the corner. Two soldiers without helmets stood there, and he jumped up and pulled the trigger on the stun gun.

Naturally, it failed to discharge. *Dammit, what the hell is this?* It had no biometric sensors to prevent him from using it; he'd checked that. And he knew it was operational since he'd almost been shot with it. They stared at him and brought their weapons up, and he threw the pistol at the one on the right as he dove into a forward somersault. It caused the man to flinch, and the laser blast missed. The other one's shot singed Jax's back as he went to the floor.

Oh, hell, guess they've decided capture is no longer a priority. Okay, that ups the ante. As he rolled to his feet, he drew one of his long knives with his right hand and tightened his grip on the mace in his left. His enemies' heads presented *such* an inviting target, especially since they were now trying to kill him. Still, they were allegedly on the same team, more or less. He whipped the spiked club up at the left one's rifle, knocked it upward, and hopefully damaged the barrel. If it had been his weapon, he certainly wouldn't feel confident shooting it after the impact, that's for sure.

He dropped to his right knee, chambered the knife across his stomach and reversed his grip, then stabbed it backhand into the right-side soldier's thigh. It pierced the armor with only a minimal reduction in velocity, and the man went down with a scream as the point came out the other side. If he were fighting an unarmored opponent, he'd have finished the blow by wrenching the blade forward to cut it free of his foe's leg, but the front leg plate would make that impossible. Instead, he released it and threw himself into a sideways roll to avoid the downward strike of the first one's rifle butt.

Athena, help me knock him out but not kill him. He leapt ahead, took a blow from the rifle on his flesh and blood arm, and hooked a punch with his left to the man's temple. He noticed a strange feeling as the AI moderated the impact's force, and the man went down. Jax repeated the process with the medkits he'd performed earlier, making sure both soldiers were stable for the moment.

Maarsen's voice was an unexpected gift. "All units, the enemies are retreating. Keep drone coverage on them, but let them go. The authorities have been summoned and will arrive shortly. Students, stay in your safe locations. Staff, conduct a sweep and ensure we've got them all. We expect to have full systems operational within the hour, so be vigilant until then."

Jax sighed in relief. "Let's get down there and make sure Juno and her colleagues are okay. Then we can move on to the problem at hand."

Athena replied, "The soldiers' source of information inside the castle."

"Yep. No doubt the Professor is doing his best, but you and I need to put our heads together and figure it out, fast."

She snorted but skipped the obvious joke about them only having one head. He cleaned and sheathed his knives, rested the mace on his right shoulder, and headed for the medical lab.

CHAPTER TWENTY-FOUR

Jax, Maarsen, Stephenson, Juno, the Academy's weapons master, and the Academy's quartermaster were seated around an oval table in a rectangular chamber he'd not seen before. Located behind the control room for the training space, it was undoubtedly the most modern thing in the castle. Even the chairs looked high tech and had proved to be so when he sat, and the seat and back conformed to his body with a brief whir of motors. Each of the walls except the one with the door had a single large curved display mounted on it. The long ones held an array of paused images from the castle's security cameras.

On the short wall behind Maarsen's position at the head of the table, the monitor showed a freeze-frame aerial view of the sedan that slammed into the lobby to kick off the assault. The dining hall crew had provided sandwiches and coffee, and as they all finished making their choices, the Professor spoke. "We have three goals to accomplish, none of which will be complete by the time we leave this room, so expect to be busy until further notice." He smiled at them, and they all laughed softly. Jax imagined the others lacked free time as much or more than he did. "First, to discuss in broad strokes the strategic and tactical objectives behind yesterday's attack on the castle, and what it means for our future operations." His face turned hard, and Jax sensed the seething anger hidden within his calm words.

"Second," he didn't quite growl, "to identify any lessons learned from their attack and our defense. Third, to discuss the possibility that there is an animate or inanimate traitor in our midst." Scowls appeared around the table, and Jax felt his lips turn down. *Although we all know there has to be one, it hurts to be forced to admit it.*

Athena offered, "It will be worse once we share our information with them."

Yes, it will. But let's listen to the others first. Maybe we're too self-centered about the whole thing. No witty comebacks, please.

"No. Not the right time."

Harrington, the weapons master he'd met while assisting in Kenton Marshall's "entrance exam" spoke first. Even sitting, he radiated energy from his compact form, somewhere about halfway between Jax's height and Cia's. As he talked, the displays slid into motion, showing the scenes he described. "The sedan was autonomous, with a decoy android in the driver's seat. It was an off-the-shelf model, based on what we were able to recover, and we're trying to track its source. The vans were local rentals. We are working with the assumption that the soldiers came down in shuttles somewhere within a couple of hours' drive, and circled to approach from different directions as they reached our outer perimeter."

Stephenson interrupted, "Which means you think they knew about your drones."

Maarsen chuckled. "We'll get there, Anika. Let Harrington finish." He leaned conspiratorially toward the person on his other side, the quartermaster, and whispered loudly enough for everyone to hear, "She's always been impulsive. Ever since she was a student."

Hellene, the Academy's quartermaster, nodded. She was probably a decade younger than Maarsen, with hair going from brown to grey pulled back in a bun. She wore the standard black uniform of the Academy's students. "I remember it well."

Harrington cleared his throat and continued. "The soldiers we detained had no identifying materials on them, and a facial recognition scan came up empty, both in our databases and in those we can access. That means we've never seen them, and someone else has been very good at covering their tracks."

Maarsen muttered, "Arlox."

The weapons master nodded. "Almost certainly this is the Intelligence Division's work. The armor was military standard, but we found no records suggesting the military purchased it. Same with the weapons."

Jax tapped the table thoughtfully. "So, all of that suggests the op was put on in kind of a hurry, right? Otherwise, they would have done a better job of laying a false trail, rather than a blank one. Maybe Confederacy gear, for instance."

Harrington shrugged. "That's my working hypothesis, yes, but it's far from confirmed. We're currently sweeping the castle to see if they left any surveillance devices behind, but none of our cameras showed such activity before they went down."

Maarsen spread his hands. "So, the question of the moment: what did they seek by the attack, why did they want to accomplish that objective, and what was effective against them? Anika, you first."

Stephenson scowled. "If it's Arlox, then it could be another move in the damned game the two of you have played for years. But if it had an additional purpose, it's probably not a coincidence that Jax was here when it happened, given the interest the Intelligence Division has previously shown in him."

Harrington offered, "I can't speak to what occurred outside the Academy. What I *can* say is that their actions weren't consistent with an intent to take and hold the facility. They would have needed five times their number at a minimum. So it was meant to be a quick hit and fade, which argues in favor of Major Stephenson's conclusion."

Hellene added, "The fact that they used non-lethal force until their comms malfunctioned is another piece of evidence supporting an intent to capture someone or something." Jax and Athena had judged they were best served by keeping her intervention with the enemy's communications secret. "The sophistication of their gear also adds weight to the notion that it was an Intelligence Division operation. The guns were tied to transponders in their gauntlets, which is why no one could use them against the intruders."

Ahh, that makes sense. Not biometric as such, but a transponder, or maybe a physical contact in the glove.

Athena sounded annoyed. "I will gather information on defeating that precaution, in case we encounter it again."

Maarsen asked, "What do you think, Jackson?"

"I agree with what everyone has said so far. I believe the operation was aimed at me, or more specifically, the AI in my skull. She agrees. It explains the numbers, the non-lethal entry, and their lack of a clear objective once they got in. We've reviewed the patterns in the camera footage, and it looks like they were searching for something. Probably me."

He received a round of nods in response. "It's more likely when you consider how much the intruders knew about the castle to begin with. Public plans are available from various moments in the building's history, naturally, although I noticed they're not quite accurate."

Maarsen laughed. "Yes, modifying them so they couldn't be used against us was one of our first counterintelligence operations. The physical originals we replaced are carefully stored in a hermetically sealed cabinet. The digital versions are preserved as well, although those are obviously of less historical value."

Jax nodded. "Right. But the way they moved suggested they were following maps in their displays, or at least had memorized the layout. They weren't discovering the spaces as they came to them; they had preassigned routes. That means they had a current map of the layout. It could have come from only a few places. First, someone could have hacked into the Academy's systems. Second, a past student or employee could have shared information or planted surveillance devices. Finally, a current student or employee could have done either of those things."

Harrington shook his head decisively. "I've checked with the computer people, and with the backup computer people, in case. Everyone agrees that no external breach of our systems occurred. Our security is at worst equivalent to, and most likely better than, anything the Alliance or Confederacy possesses."

"Athena and I figured that would be the case, but it's still nice to hear it confirmed. So, that leaves former people or present people as reasonable vectors for information to have gotten out. I mean, sure, they could be drilling under us right now with some fantastical device, but it seems unlikely."

Harrington muttered, "The seismic sensors would notice that," but it was clear his concern had moved on to the idea that someone had betrayed them. "Sounds as if we'll have to investigate our own."

Maarsen cautioned, "First, I think we need to narrow the possibilities. Are we agreed that we're proceeding as if Jackson is the target?" More nods, with Major Stephenson's the most emphatic. "All right. Then we can limit our pool to those who knew about his current visit. I can vet the former students and former employees."

Jax interrupted, "There's another factor to consider." The Professor gestured for him to continue. "It probably has to be a person who knows about Athena. It would explain most simply how Arlox found out."

The quartermaster offered, "Occam's Razor in action. Sure. That makes a lot of sense."

Maarsen shook his head, but it wasn't a negation, it was regret. "That means it's someone close. The only potential employees would be the medical staff."

Jax frowned since unfortunately, the conclusions he and Athena had reached together had held up to the others' inquiry. "And the most likely students, in fact, the only students, would be those on my team. Cia, Kimmel, Sirenno, Verrand, and Marshall."

Silence reigned for several moments while they digested that notion. Harrington broke it. "Okay, that's a place to start. We'll need to trace their movements and actions. Which of them has been present during this visit?"

Stephenson growled, "All of them, at one time or another. The only ones here for the attack were Cia and Sirenno."

Athena asked, "Have your suspects changed order?"

No. Marshall, then Sirenno, Verrand, and Kimmel.

"Not Cia?"

It's not Cia. No chance. "If you'll send Athena and me the data, we can work with it as well. Multiple sets of eyes will have a better chance."

Maarsen asked, "Why? That's the real question here, right? Why would someone do this? Maybe if we figure that out, it will provide insight into who it might be."

Stephenson's tone was flat. "It always comes down to politics, money, power, or sex. Not necessarily in that order."

Harrington nodded. "Unless you're dealing with a sociopath, in which case no rules apply, but I agree. And the students we bring in often have drives in more than one of those areas. It's that broad desire for accomplishment that allows them to become successful in the first place."

Jax hadn't considered the situation through those lenses

yet. He was still in the information-gathering phase and didn't like to color the data collection by being overly focused on the results. In this case, that was more difficult than usual. *Because the betrayal is personal, maybe deeply so.*

Athena sounded uncertain. "The others have shifted their attention to your team. I feel that I must remind you that everyone in the medical lab is also a potential subject. Including Dr. Cray."

I know. The possibility that our relationship is some sort of elaborate honeypot has crossed my mind, but honestly, I think it ranks somewhere pretty close to Cia on the "no way" scale. But since I will clearly have a blind spot there, I'll trust you to make your own judgment. You have my express permission to use my comm to send a message to Stephenson if you think I'm irrational.

"I *always* think you're irrational. It's one of your most appealing features. And while I don't technically need your permission, thank you for the thought."

Maarsen said, "Okay. Sounds like we know what we need to know to proceed. Everyone get going on your research. I have a party to throw together for Friday, which means we'll have all the likely suspects here in three days. That's how long you have to figure it out."

CHAPTER TWENTY-FIVE

By the time the night of the party arrived, Jax and the others had narrowed it down to two. Cia was above suspicion for him from the start and was cleared by the investigation as he'd expected. In the case of Ethan Kimmel, Jax thought he was probably too young and innocent to be a double agent. But they'd done their due diligence and discovered that he was exactly what he seemed: brilliant, earnest, awkward, and trustworthy.

Clearing Sirenno was harder since his movements proved difficult to track. Eventually, their surveillance uncovered that he was dating several people who didn't know about one another, and his shifty moves and secretive ways were attributable to that circumstance.

Everyone in the medical lab had checked out, so that left Maria Verrand and Kenton Marshall. His money was on Marshall, but he wasn't sure how much he wanted that to be the case since he trusted the man less than Verrand. Athena had pointed out to Jax that he probably had some transference going on, assigning positive qualities to the woman based on his knowledge of Beatrice O'Leary. It was potentially a legitimate blind spot, so she didn't exit the list.

Marshall's personality was spiky, and that seemed to fit the idea of a traitor pretty well. Jax recognized that particular argument's speciousness and had dug into him and his company as much as possible. But after all of their efforts, it could still be either of them. *Or someone else entirely, that we're not seeing.*

They would strip away whatever privacy remained to the pair by planting bugs in their comms and detailing teams of watchers to keep an eye on them at the party. That would go on for as long as required to discover who had betrayed them. Jax was decidedly not interested in waiting. He was determined to figure out which of them was guilty or clear them both before the end of the night.

The party would be the perfect place for him to chat individually with each of his team members. He hadn't seen any of them in a while, other than Cia, and looked forward to catching up. His connection to them would make confirming that one of them was a traitor all the more painful.

Strands of hanging lights, tents, buffet tables, and a string quartet playing in one corner decorated the castle's "backyard," which played host to the event. He'd opted for the black suit and no tie look again and sauntered over to Juno, who hobnobbed with her people. "Hello, beautiful."

She grinned at him. "Hello, yourself. It seems like you need to go clothes shopping. I've seen that outfit."

He nodded. "Definitely a good point. Your dress is

gorgeous, as always." She wore a shimmering blue sheath that covered too much of her for Jax's taste.

She frowned and pulled him aside. "You seem off. What's up?"

He looked down at the grass, idly wondering how they kept it so lush in the Northern Scotland climate. "Tonight's a work night for me, unfortunately. And I'm not looking forward to what I have to do."

Her hand found his and squeezed it. "Maarsen told me. I'll be nearby whenever I can be if you need an assist."

He chuckled. "The Professor is pulling all of our strings, isn't he?"

"He is. But at least he's doing it in the service of a good cause, right?"

"I certainly hope so. If not, he might become a supervillain. Which would make the castle his lair. And you a flunky."

She shook her head. "At minimum, I'm a henchwoman."

Jax shrugged. "I'll give you minion, tops." His attention was drawn away by his team's entrance, all five of whom walked in together. He'd wanted to let Cia in on the plan before tonight, but everyone had argued against it. Jax was sure she'd be able to pretend well enough to fool the rest— he'd seen her in action with her family, after all—but he didn't feel like fighting about it. *If she gets upset, I'll point her at Maarsen, and he can deal with her.*

Athena laughed. "You think that will work, do you?"

Probably not. Are you ready to handle their comms?

"Of course." The Academy's programmers had given the AI the codes to the full network, and she would use that access to hack the comms of their suspects. She'd pull whatever data she could during the evening, but needed him to get close enough that she could perform the initial breach using both the wireless network and the comms' near field communication, which was often much faster. Otherwise, the security features their companies had doubtless loaded onto their devices might prove a problem. *And if one of them has an Intelligence Division comm in disguise, it'll be even more challenging.*

Athena scoffed, "Hardly. I could do it over the wireless no matter what, but it's true that the chance of discovery is slightly smaller this way. You all are astonishingly risk-averse." He laughed as he thought of how unsafe his everyday life was, then headed for the group. He greeted each of them individually, then pulled Cia away from the bunch. The AI asked, "Are you sure about this? Everyone else disagrees."

Yes.

"It's not required."

It is for me. "Cia, I have something to tell you, and I don't think you're going to like it." Even condensed, their suspicions took several minutes to explain. The tension in her body language increased with each one that passed. When he finished, she shook her head.

"I can't believe it. That's crazy. I mean, we've trusted them with our lives."

Jax swept his gaze over the crowd. He had decided at the last minute not to wear the display glasses to avoid spooking his targets, who would doubtless recognize them for what they were. But that meant he had to keep an eye on them normally, and they'd split apart to socialize. "I agree. But how much do we really know about anyone here? Take a slow look around. They're each talking to someone I can't name right now. Which suggests a whole web of connections we're unaware of." Athena knew as much about their personal networks as anyone at the Academy, thanks to the data that Harrington had provided for her to analyze, but none had offered any additional insight. Whoever the mole was, they were good at it. *Which is all the more frustrating.*

She did as he asked and put a goofy smile on her face to conceal her feelings. When she completed her scan, she shook her head again. "You're right. But I still can't see it."

"I've had some time to get used to the idea. Plus, you know, being the target of a major assault tends to make one less trusting."

She laughed darkly. "Was my presence at the castle during the attack a point in my favor?"

He shrugged. "I can't speak for anyone else, but I never included you among the possibilities. If you're the one, I'll eat my helmet. If I'm that easy to fool, I don't deserve to wear it. You're not exactly subtle, after all." She laughed, harder than required, and he realized why as Maria Verrand stepped into their circle. *Thanks for the warning.*

Athena replied, "Cia had you covered. I saw her spot Verrand on an incoming vector when she surveyed the crowd."

You're getting overconfident.

"An impossibility."

Jax allowed the grin to reach his lips, knowing Verrand would probably think it was because of Cia's laughter, and turned to face the new arrival. "Maria. Good to see you." They exchanged fist bumps, and the two women did the same. Verrand looked paler than usual like she might be fighting off a cold.

Cia inquired, "What have you been up to?"

Verrand sighed. "The usual. Work and more work, with vacations to do work for the Academy."

Jax laughed. "You're aware that being part of Azophi is optional, right?"

She nodded. "Yeah, but leaving now that I know about the place is impossible. A challenge like this? If you don't beat it, it'll haunt you." A hint of pain colored her words. *Athena, anything in her background that includes some pivotal failure?*

"Negative. By all accounts, she's overcome every problem she's faced professionally. Interpersonal relationships are average. Your type of people tends to attract partners easily, but find keeping them difficult. Something to think about, maybe."

Shut it.

Verrand gave him a small smile. "Talking to your passenger?"

Interesting that she noticed that. "Yes. She's explaining to me that I should break up with Juno before I infect her with a case of terminal stupidity."

The women laughed as if they believed him, and Athena replied, "I said no such thing. However, it's good that you've arrived at that truth on your own."

Yeah, yeah. How's the breach going?

"Already inside and planting our tracers. Another minute should do it."

Cia made an excuse and headed off into the crowd, and he asked Verrand, "So, not to be overly inquisitive, but you seem more on edge than usual. Anything I can help you with?" He wouldn't have seen it if he hadn't been paying extra attention to nonverbal cues, but the clues to her stress were there in her body language—the slightly too upright stance, the hint of a wince at the corners of her eyes, the way her open hand kept balling into a fist.

She sighed. "It's nothing. A relationship that's about to explode, plus a busy time at work with a new contract. You know how it is."

Athena murmured, "Checking." They'd already been over everything, so she wasn't likely to find new information, but it certainly didn't hurt to look.

"So, nothing I can help with since I'm not smart enough for logistics and have a history of failed relationships that's doubtless far more impressive than yours."

She laughed, and it seemed only half-forced. "Oh, I think there might be a competition there."

He nodded and drew her slightly away from the rest of the crowd. *Okay, here we go.* "Listen, I'm sure you heard about the attack on the Academy, right?"

"Of course. It's all anyone who was here for it is talking about. Have they found out who was behind it?"

"Leading candidate is someone named Arlox, from the Intelligence Division." She looked away before responding. *Damn it, Maria. That's one strike.*

Her eyes rose to his again. "Why them?"

He shrugged. "I don't fully know the reasoning. Stephenson and Maarsen have taken the lead on it, and I'm aware the Professor has a long-standing thing with the head of intelligence." *Which is putting it rather mildly.* "What I want to know is what the point of it was. Any ideas?"

She frowned. "They haven't said? No, I guess they haven't if you're wondering. Sorry. I'm a little off because of the stuff at home. I'd hoped that the party here would take my mind off it." Verrand paused, and he saw the moment that she regained control of her expression, forcing a concerned look onto it to replace the worried one that had been there. The difference was subtle, but he recognized the transition from inward-focus to outward-focus from other interrogations he'd been part of. "I'd guess it's aimed at the Professor, then. We probably triggered the Intelligence Division when we snatched up the AI. They have to be concerned about that."

He nodded. "Yeah, I thought about that. Athena accused me of being self-centered." He forced a laugh appropriate to the statement. "But how would they know it was me? I can't see the Confederacy or the Alien Coalition calling up Arlox or whoever and saying, 'Hey, did one of yours steal something from us? Could we have it back, please?' Doesn't make sense."

The ice in the drink she held clinked as a tremor ran through her hand. *Hell. Strike two.* She replied, "Good point. I don't know. I hope we're safe now." That rang true, although she might have referred to herself and not to the Academy. Her eyes were roving, clearly looking for an escape. "Oh, there's someone I haven't seen forever. I'll talk to you later, Jax."

He turned to watch her go and kept his face steadily neutral. *She's at the top of the list now. But let's find Marshall and make certain of it.*

CHAPTER TWENTY-SIX

Jax found Kenton Marshall chatting with Harrington. He stepped forward to join them, and the Academy's weapons master welcomed him. "Jax, we were reflecting on the battle you two fought on Kenton's first day."

Marshall nodded. His physique had a lot in common with Jax' since they were both ex-military, and his hair was cut only slightly longer than regulation. "We need to have a rematch one of these days. With fewer restrictions."

Jax grinned. "You've been itching for a fight since that day, Kenton. I'm happy to oblige, once we get past the current, uh, unpleasantness."

Harrington explained, "Jax was right in the thick of things during the assault on the castle. He's been through a *ton* of debriefings about what happened after the cameras went down."

Anger took over Marshall's face. "I wish I'd been here. Bastards deserved a lot worse than they got. Will we go after whoever was behind it?"

Jax shrugged. "I do what they tell me, although I can say

that Maarsen is pretty fired up about it. He thinks it's an old rival of his."

"Well, then we should pay that rival a visit and punch him in the face for it."

What do you think, Athena, too over the top?

"So far it seems consistent with all the recorded behavior I have access to."

Yeah. He's a hothead. "I'd like nothing more. Harrington, have you figured out what they were after yet?" Jax had shared his plan with the others, so they knew his strategy's broad strokes, which included keeping that particular detail secret.

The weapons master shrugged. "Leading theory is that it was a challenge to the Professor, or more likely a warning. We've increased our surveillance of Intelligence Division members over the last month or so, and it's always possible we failed to be completely hidden while we did so."

Marshall growled, "Well when you know who did it, put me on the team that goes to get payback." He blew out a frustrated breath and asked in a lower voice, "Jax, how's the head?"

Annoying as ever. "She's fine. Still slowly sending threads through my whole body so she can turn me into a slave to her will. I was thinking of asking Dr. Cray to put a failsafe explosive in my neck in case I suddenly go evil."

The other men laughed, and Athena replied, "I could deactivate an implanted bomb with ease. And besides, I thought you were against that idea."

Whatever. I'll surely sleep better knowing that my offhanded comment about becoming a zombie under your control is something you've considered. Fantastic. "Seriously, though, it's fine. We still have some boundary issues here and there, but I think in the end she'll be a pretty solid asset. Especially given that we're stuck with one another, regardless."

Athena added, "Only until you die. Then I can get a better host to control."

Marshall's expression seemed sincere. "That's good to hear. It's been on my mind since the moment I hit the button to activate the implant sequence. I mean, you have. You both." He laughed in exasperation. "I don't know what I mean, apparently. But I *am* sure that I need another drink. Talk to you later?"

Jax nodded. "Definitely." The other man left, and Harrington met Jax's eyes and gave a small head shake. Jax murmured, "Agreed," then headed over to talk to Coach, who held court with seven or eight laughing students around him. *Athena, keep an eye on them both. Let me know if either does anything suspicious. We'll give them until the end of the night to incriminate themselves and decide what to do after that if they don't.*

"Got it, Jax. Just so you're aware, I am programmatically incapable of betraying you."

He chuckled inwardly. *That's good to know, Athena.*

The rest of the party offered no additional insight. He'd hoped that Verrand would do something to earn her that third strike so he could be sure she was the one before he took action, but she hadn't. Of course, if the traitor were smart, they would work very hard at appearing innocent, given the recent activities.

He activated the plan he and Athena had worked up. The AI had recorded Stephenson's lines earlier since the Major had left before the party began. His team's comms signaled an alert, followed by Stephenson's voice, angry and urgent. "Jackson, this message is going to your entire team. We've discovered you were the target of the attack and that the Intelligence Division carried it out by working on information supplied from *inside* the Academy. That means you and your team are in danger. All of you head to your quarters and await further instructions while we nail down who did it."

Jax snapped across the channel that connected them all, "Acknowledged, Major. Reese out. People, get to your rooms, double time." He followed his orders, then slipped on his display glasses and laid back on the bed. Small dots on a map of the castle's floor plan indicated the location of the Academy comms that each of his team members wore, showing them all in their quarters. He muttered, "Now we wait. Athena, wake me if something useful happens." She had access to the Academy's entire security system for this operation and would know immediately.

An undetermined amount of time later, she woke him with an alarm that ramped up gently from nothingness. He was alert before it reached half-volume. "What?"

"Motion sensors outside Verrand's window have been activated. Also, her personal comm shows her beyond the walls. She appears to be wearing a camouflage suit since neither thermal detection nor cameras have spotted her."

Jax shot out of his bed, grabbed his stun pistol and

medkit, and burst from his room. *What direction is she heading?*

"The road. Front side exit is your most efficient choice."

He pounded down the corridor toward the indicated door. *Alert the security staff at the road.* They'd detailed several staff members to serve as guards around the castle for the evening of the party, and they'd moved to concealed positions to continue their duty into the night. *Any action on the drones?*

"Normal traffic for this time of night. One motorcycle, three cars, and a cargo truck."

Damn it. Maarsen needs to get some weaponized versions, whether it makes him feel uncomfortable or not. Did you find anything in Verrand's background to suggest she's an agent?

"Nothing. Gifted amateur at best, to use your words."

He chuckled inwardly at the memory of describing his Academy team that way to her. In truth, they were *very* gifted, but for combat situations didn't begin to approach the level of his Special Forces unit. *Okay, vector me in behind her. I'm going to guess I can move more quietly than she can. If she seems like she reacts to my presence, do that thing with the comms again if you can.*

"That will reveal it was us who did it during the attack."

Can't be helped. She's not getting away. At least we probably don't have to worry about anything stupid like a suicide pill, since she's likely not an agent.

Athena gave a small snort. "That's a lot of 'probably,' Jax."

Yeah. Hope for the best, plan for the worst. Give me a path. A line appeared on the ground ahead in his display, showing him the quietest approach with the best footing, in the AI's estimation. He followed it and spotted the telltale smear of Verrand's camouflage suit as she crouched near the road. *Connect me to her personal comm.*

"Done."

He raised the pistol and aimed it at Verrand's spine. In a whisper, so he didn't give away his position, he ordered, "Maria. You're not going to make it. Deactivate the suit, take off your helmet, and put your hands on the back of your head. Do it now." She jumped up and tried to run. He pulled the trigger and bathed her in a wide-beam stun blast. She fell, and he rushed to her side and removed the helmet to be sure she was still breathing. He injected her with a sedative and sighed. "Damn it, Maria. Strike three."

The castle didn't have anything like an interrogation cell. The prisoner holding it did have in the basement was from a time long past, and inadequate to their needs. Guards had carried the unconscious woman to the medical unit, where Juno and her team put her in a safe set of clothes. They strapped her down to one of the operating tables, and Maarsen shooed everyone out of the room other than Jax, Juno, and himself.

He instructed, "Go ahead and wake her up." Juno tapped a button on her tablet, and a robot arm descended and injected a stim into Verrand's neck. The woman's eyes flew open, and she tried to sit up, only to discover that she was immobile.

Tears gathered, and she shook her head. "I'm sorry. I didn't want to. I didn't *mean* to." One escaped to slide down the side of her face and drop onto the tile floor. "I had no choice."

Jax's voice held no sympathy. "You could have come to me."

She shook her head again. "No. They were always watching, always listening." She thrashed. "Wait, you talked to me over my personal comm. They'll have heard it. They're going to kill my sister."

Maarsen snapped, "Name."

"Carlie Cassel. She's married. Lives in the United States."

The professor stepped off to the side and spoke urgently into his comm. Juno reassured her, "We'll find her and protect her. It's only been twenty minutes; it will be some time before they can get the pieces in place to take action. The Intelligence Division is behind this, right?"

Maria nodded and mastered her tears with a visible effort of will. "Yes. Bastards."

Jax urged, "What happened, Maria? Tell us all of it."

She sniffed, but anger had replaced her moment of weakness. "After the mission where you wound up with Athena in your head, I went back to work. Things were normal for a few days. Then I was taken on the way home. There's no other word for it. One minute I was stepping into an empty car for my commute, and the next I woke up in a bare room with bright lights everywhere." A shiver passed through her at the memory. "They explained that they knew about my boyfriend, knew about my sister, and knew about my presence at the Academy. I was to be their inside person, and I would be watched from then on to ensure compliance. Failure would result in the deaths of those I loved. No second chances."

Jax understood why she hadn't spoken up. His response might have been different, but he had a far greater number of resources to throw at the problem, including at least one Special Forces unit. "So why aren't we tracking down your boyfriend?"

She growled, "I broke up with him so they wouldn't need to kill him. Better me hurting him than them ending his life."

"And maybe hurting yourself felt right, too."

She nodded. "Could be. I'm worthless."

He reached forward and undid the top strap holding her in place. "No, you're human, and you got played by people with more power than you. Happens a lot. That's not on you unless you want it to be."

Juno gave him a warning glare, and he responded with a slight shake of his head. "I believe you, Maria. Now, understand that we'll be watching you too, from here on out. Chances are good that they'll know you're burnt and leave you alone, but you'll need to take precautions until we bring them down."

She scowled. "Bastards deserve to go down hard."

He undid the last strap. "And they will. Count on it. Now, Dr. Cray is going to spend some time with you, and probably Professor Maarsen too, checking your story and making sure that they didn't do anything else to you while you were in their hands that you don't know about." She paled a little at his words. "After that, you're still welcome on the team, once you've told the others what happened."

"Do you think you can ever trust me again?"

He smiled. "Maria, I wouldn't have invited you back if I didn't already trust you. Everyone makes mistakes. Yours was big, but that's what happens in the major leagues, and that's where we're playing. You deserve the chance to make it right."

Maarsen returned. "Your sister and her family are safe. Local authorities have taken them to a secure spot, and one of our students who is also a principal in a security company will take care of them from there. The Academy will ensure their relocation and new identities, along with something equivalent to the jobs and lives they had before."

She nodded. "Thank you. Thank you all. I'm sorry. But I'm going to make up for it. Promise."

Athena offered, "I believe her."

Me too. Now let's see about finding her a target.

CHAPTER TWENTY-SEVEN

An hour later, they were seated around the table in the office behind the training room's operations station again. Only this time, Stephenson was participating as a giant head on the display behind Maarsen instead of in person.

She growled, "So, we know it was the Intelligence Division, which means we know it was Arlox."

Maarsen lifted a hand. "Well, we know that Maria Verrand *thinks* it was the Intelligence Division, which if true *probably* means Arlox is responsible."

Jax's snort was only an instant before Stephenson's. *Maybe satellite delay between here and the* Cronus. He said, "Let's let the half-a-percent chance that it isn't Arlox and the Intelligence Division go. We know it's them. For a hundred different reasons, it has to be them. So, the question is, how do we move forward?"

Harrington shrugged. "Our computer people have a way into the Intelligence Division's network, but we haven't been able to access anything beyond the outermost level. That gives us virtually nothing other than a little assistance with tracking their agents.

The quartermaster, Hellene, observed, "We've tried on several occasions to get a physical tap into their systems, but their defenses are too good for that." *Huh. Maybe they're the Academy's spymasters together? That's an interesting idea.*

Jax said, "I think we have a solution there, but Athena and I wanted to be sure that everyone was okay with it."

Maarsen replied, "Do tell, Jackson."

He smiled. "I'll let her explain." An image of a woman's head and neck appeared on one of the displays. She had long blonde hair, a sharp nose, and ears that seemed almost pointed at the top. Jax figured she'd taken the look from an ancient picture of the Greek goddess Athena and modified it to her liking. Her voice came out of the speakers as the image spoke.

"I used the surveillance connection from Maria Verrand's comm to hook into their systems. They haven't yet shut it down, which is to our advantage, but I cannot imagine that will hold for long. As it's possible that they might, in turn, trace the path back to here, I would prefer permission before attempting to break into their network."

Maarsen looked at Harrington, who looked at Hellene with a nod. She said, "You have it. We'll deal with any fall-out. It's not like they're filled with overwhelming goodwill toward us at the moment anyway."

Jax nodded. "Show us what you've got, Athena."

The display blanked for a moment, then a scroll of data began. She said through the speakers, "I am in the outer network. Negotiating for access to the internal network." After a pause, she added, "Into the internal network. Security responding." The data on the screen flowed faster. "Disconnecting."

In all, it took fifteen seconds. Maarsen asked, "Did you get anything? Did they backtrace it to the Academy?"

Athena's face reappeared on the display. "No, Professor, they did not identify us. The connection routed through thirty-seven hubs, and I killed it after they reached number thirty." She vanished, and filenames appeared where she'd been. "I was able to copy four thousand, seven hundred, and twenty-eight files."

The humans in the room broke into applause, and Stephenson grinned from her display. Maarsen instructed, "All right. Let's all get some sleep. Jackson, we'll meet after the analysts have gone through the files. Well done, everyone."

Well done, Athena. Also, I love the look you've chosen.

She sounded satisfied and pleased. "Thank you on both accounts, Jax."

The trove of information had revealed several important clues, and Stephenson had made the trip to Earth to take part in the planning session that they inspired, which delayed their meeting until the afternoon. That was fine by Jax since he used the time to stock up on sleep. When he arrived at the office, a third chair had been pulled up on the far side of Maarsen's desk, and Cia walked into the room after him. She quipped, "Wow, you can almost smell the burning of the big brains at work."

Maarsen chuckled. "Indeed, and one hopes they are

more adequate to the task ahead than they have been to the ones behind."

Jax grinned at his teammate. "Now that Cia's here, nothing can stop us from coming up with the best ideas in the universe."

She stuck out her tongue at him as she took the center seat. On her right, Stephenson nodded a greeting. "Pilot."

Cia replied, "Boss lady," and everyone laughed.

The Professor said, "Okay. Here's where we stand. First, we've confirmed that there is a second traitor, this time to the UCCA rather than directly to the Academy." He lifted his chin a little and spoke to the air. "Activate display." A holographic image of some of the data Athena had stolen appeared over his desk. "As you can see, the Intelligence Division is after this individual as well. However, they're hampered by their methods, which focus on direct action, interrogation, and the like."

Stephenson interjected, "Well, to be fair, those are usually pretty effective."

Maarsen nodded. "Of course, of course. But for this situation, where we're having problems finding the right haystack to look in, much less tracking down the proper needle, the Academy's resources are more appropriate. We put out a quiet word and got back a plethora of rumors and observations, most of which led nowhere. But a few of them pointed in the same direction. One more question to the right people gave us a potential location for the person feeding information about Jackson to the Confederacy."

The older man paused dramatically, and Jax sighed. "Don't keep us in suspense, Professor."

Stephenson growled, "Out with it, Nikolai."

Cia laughed. "Oh, torture them both some more. This is fun."

A chuckle preceded the revelation. "Tortuga."

Stephenson and Jax shook their heads at the name, but Cia groaned. "Not Tortuga. Why did it have to be Tortuga?" He couldn't tell if she was joking or not, which probably meant she was serious since subtlety wasn't exactly her thing.

Athena offered, "I can tell you all about Tortuga."

Later. Let's see what Maarsen has to say. "I presume you're going to give us more than a name, Professor?"

He nodded. "Display the Quni system." A bright sun appeared first, then four planets with lines representing their elliptical orbits around it faded into existence. They moved slowly along their gravitationally bound paths and spun in place as they inched ahead. "Zoom in on the fourth planet." The display complied and revealed a world covered in white, its distance from the star rendering it frozen and uninhabitable. Three moons hung above its surface, and one of them had another object hovering over it that seemed to hold a geosynchronous position relative to the larger body.

Jax observed, "I take it that thing is Tortuga?"

Cia nodded. "Yes. It is not a nice place. Not at all. On the one hand, you have the kind of pirates who are out to make a living by skirting the law a little. Like those we ran into on Sapphire station. These aren't them. These are the real baddies, who delight in extreme mayhem. When they take a break from all the murdering and plundering, they stay aboard the *Tortuga*."

The image zoomed in again to show that what he'd

thought was a medium-sized ship was actually one of the biggest the UCCA had. "How the hell did pirates get their hands on a freaking battleship?"

Stephenson explained, "I remember something about this. I think the decision had been made to scuttle it, but a particularly motivated pirate clan killed the demolition team and took their places. They managed to get it stable enough to tow to the nearest defensible position, then added weapons to protect it. The whole system is supposed to be mined, as I recall." She shook her head. "I'll pull the relevant information for you. But the ship isn't viable now as anything other than a base of operations, so we tend not to care too much about it."

Cia scowled. "Well, while you've been not caring, the pirates turned it into one of the worst places in the universe. And you're telling me we have to go there?"

Maarsen gave an apologetic shrug. "That's where the evidence is leading us. Whatever the UCCA traitor is up to, it's somehow connected to the *Tortuga*."

Jax chuckled darkly. "I don't suppose you can whip up a dozen assault teams on short notice, Major?"

"You have no idea how much I'd like to. But no, I can't. At best, I can probably provide a diversion. A show of force to get them looking away from you. Although that carries the risk of amping up their defenses right when you're making a play."

Cia added, "Speaking of which, how the *hell* are we going to get in there and find what we need?"

Three heads swiveled toward Jax. He shrugged. "I guess it's time for us to become pirates."

They'd spent hours working out the plan's details, took a break for dinner, then gathered again to poke holes in it. Everyone agreed that the timetable required at least three days of preparation before they made their move, and that was pushing it right up to the limit. None of them argued against the need to act quickly.

Another night's sleep and Jax was ready for what lay ahead. He and Athena had dispatched a message to the quartermaster the night before to ensure the items his team required for the operation were sent on to the *Grace*. The van ride up to the airfield was quiet, his people clearly injured by Verrand's communications with the Intelligence Division despite the fact that she'd been in a situation with no good options. He let it cook while they boarded the ship and allowed it to simmer a little more as they took off and headed for the jump point.

When Cia could leave the piloting duties to Trianna, he summoned them all to the galley. *Time to lance the wound.* He cleared his throat to capture their attention. "There's no denying that all of this sucks. Arlox managing to blackmail Maria into leaking information? Sucks. Having to go up against pirates on their home turf? Sucks. Knowing that the government most of us have trusted to a greater or lesser extent is fallible to the machinations of evil people within it? Sucks." He shook his head. "Having to fly on the gods-damned *Jigsaw* again? *Totally* sucks."

He got the laugh he expected, although it was far less mirthful than it would have been in just about any other situation. *Baby steps.* "But we have some things working in our favor, too. Things that will tip the balance in our direction. We've protected Maria's family, so she's back with us. More, we were able to use the Intelligence idiots' play against them and get a line on the next piece of the puzzle."

He paced slowly, wanting them to stay focused on him. "We have the backing of the Special Forces, and they're ready to cause a distraction to help us if we need it. Sure, they probably have an angle, but as long as it works out right for everyone except the pirates, it's all good. Plus, they'll be there to pull us out of the fire if things go wrong."

Cia nodded in response to his words, instinctively knowing the others would look at her for confirmation. Pilots always had power, even when they weren't also shipmasters like Cia was. Athena said, "She's very good."

She is. We're fortunate to have her on our side. Imagine if she had gone pirate? He snorted inwardly. *I bet she'd be one of the most flamboyant and fierce buccaneers the universe has ever seen.* "Finally, we have each other. We're going to have to breach the ship's physical security, and Marshall and I are pretty proficient in that area. We'll need to compromise their systems and look for clues, and all of you have talents there. Plus, we have a wild card." He tapped his temple. "Those pirates won't know what hit them."

He sensed the mood shifting from negative to slightly positive and knew he'd accomplished all he could at the moment. "Now, rest up, review the plans for the *Tortuga*, and get ready. When we finish, we'll be on the trail of the traitor. If we're lucky, he'll lead us back to Zavian bloody Arlox, and we'll get the chance to put his face in the dirt too. Either way, we'll have taken one more step toward freeing the UCCA from those who would do us harm."

He grinned. "Now I'm going to go try to convince Trianna to talk to me. I mean, how can she resist this charm?" This time, the laughter was real, and he headed for the pilot's compartment to convince the woman to break her silence.

CHAPTER TWENTY-EIGHT

Two days later, aboard the *Jigsaw*, Jax brought his team together for a final briefing. They'd abandoned anything that could tie them to the UCCA on the *Grace* and now looked like a passably ragtag crew of miscreants. The ship's hold was filled with items purportedly stolen during raids. In fact, they'd "pirated" the cargo from a Rearden trade vessel after the Professor had paid for it in full.

The ship itself was functionally better than it had been the last time he was on board and didn't seem likely to shake itself apart at any moment. *Of course, we're not in atmosphere, either.*

Athena observed, "Nor will you be unless something goes terribly wrong."

Fair point. Cosmetically, though, the vessel looked appropriately beaten and abused. They counted on their disguises more than usual since the Academy didn't have deep access to the pirate guilds' organizational arrangement. Fortunately, clans rose and fell rapidly within the broader structure, which would help them shunt away any initial suspicion. Their story would be that they were a small trade crew that simply couldn't handle the corporate world anymore. A false trail had been laid for the ship's activities, and since that was outside the pirates' records, it *should* stand up to inspection.

Unfortunately, they couldn't exactly board the *Tortuga* with rifles in hand. Everything they could find on the place suggested that tradition permitted a blade, a pistol, and nothing more. Of course, the Academy quartermaster had done her regular amazing job and provided several additional, innocent-looking items. They each carried a scuffed multi-tool clipped to their gun belt, common the universe over. Their version included cunningly concealed computer adapters and a currently deactivated wireless connection to Jax's comm so Athena could use them. The others had disguised items, but they were all in case of unexpected trouble: lock picks, single charge stunners, and the like. He didn't think they'd come into play since the operation would either be very quiet or very loud, with little room for subtlety in the latter circumstance.

Jax carried several gadgets that would be of greater use. He wore a notably expensive brand of display glasses, but if anyone but him tried them on, they would show only blurry information. He'd admit that he was trying to look impressive, but they were all image and no function. A small pouch held a pack of thin cigars and a lighter. Half of the cigars were real; the others were part of an explosive mixture. The other component was disguised as a spare magazine for his pistol. How much gel he put on the thin tubes would determine the delay until it detonated. The best part was that when separated, neither registered as dangerous on any scan.

Finally, he wore a scuffed and scratched coin around his neck as a good luck charm. In reality, it was an emergency beacon to call in backup. He'd spent over an hour debating the pros and cons with Stephenson but had agreed to take it in the end. Her position was that the UCCA was well within its rights to harass the pirates and that no particular political fallout would result from doing so. He was concerned that she was willing to fall on her sword, professionally speaking, to protect him and his team. He planned not to have to use it. Still, if he were completely honest, having the option made him feel more confident than he would have without it.

He looked around at the faces staring back at him and smiled in satisfaction. "You are a bunch of scurvy dogs, you are." They laughed and did their pirate imitations. "Okay, so, one more time through the plan. We're normal pirates looking for some rest, recreation, and trade. We'll stick together as best we can, but if we get separated, our comms' encryption should allow us to keep our communication secret." The devices on their wrists appeared ordinary on the outside, but were as high tech on the inside as his military version, according to the quartermaster. "If we are split, we work in teams. Me and Cia, Maria and Ethan, Anton and Kenton." They nodded as he said their names.

"Primary objective is getting the information and getting out alive. If it turns out that the traitor is on board the *Tortuga*, we'll improvise. Unless threatened with immediate harm, we do everything we can to avoid going loud. But if we do have to go loud, no quarter for anyone who opposes us. Cia says these folks are the worst kind of people, the ones who will kill the crew of a surrendered ship for sport." He shook his head. "It'll be hard not to be provoked if they're as bad as she claims. But we need to keep our focus pure. Get in. Get the stuff. Get out." He chuckled inwardly. *Where have I heard that before?*

Athena replied, "Every mission for the Academy so far, I believe. Apparently, you're a one-trick pony to them."

Yeah, but I'm excellent at that one trick. "Questions?"

Maria Verrand, who appeared to have apologized her way back into the others' good graces, asked, "What's the exit plan if we get separated?"

Cia replied, "Anyone who can get to the *Jigsaw* should. I've shown Ethan enough about flying that he should be able to get clear and hit the autopilot to get to jump range if I'm not here."

Jax nodded. "And those who can't get back to the *Jigsaw* should fade into the background. Everyone has sufficient cash to last a week or two aboard the ship if they're careful. Something this big, there are certain to be places to go to ground. Anyone who gets out can call in the cavalry. Major Stephenson's connection is in your comm under 'Mom.'" They laughed. "If no one gets out, I'll be the one calling for help."

Verrand shrugged. "Sounds good."

Ethan Kimmel frowned. "Does it seem to anyone else like we should have more information going in?"

Everyone made noises or gestures of agreement, including Jax. He added, "From what I hear, the interior changes a lot. It's like a city in there, but one without any real central authority. The ones in charge put down fights when they get big and keep people from drilling holes in the outer skin and decompressing the ship, but that's about as far as their concern goes. Sounds like it's as close to anarchy as anything I've ever seen."

Cia nodded. "That's what I've heard, too. Not too many pirates mess with the Rearden Company, mainly because we have a bunch of them on the payroll. It's certainly easier to tell us stuff than try to take down our ships, which almost always have hidden surprises for any attacker. But they've all been pretty clear about the fact that the *Tortuga* is not a place for the faint of heart."

Anton Sirenno lifted a palm to indicate he wanted to speak. Jax replied, "Really? Okay, please."

The other man laughed. "I'm positive my heart is weakening by the second. When we arrive, it will probably be faint. You all go ahead, don't worry about me. I'll hold down the ship."

The others laughed, and Kenton Marshall threw a wadded-up napkin at Sirenno's head. Jax answered, "Yeah, yeah, we'd all like to sit this one out, believe me. But our best chance is to go in together because we are far more potent as a group than as individuals. Any other *actual* concerns?"

None were registered, and Jax nodded. "Okay, people. Let's do this."

***

He was in the copilot's chair for the approach to the *Tortuga*. As it grew larger in the display, the extensive damage the ship had taken during whatever battle had put it out of commission became visible. Jax breathed, "Holy hell," as he zoomed the image in and scrolled it along the vessel's side. It appeared as if no more than a single panel or two of the original hull had survived in any given place, and the beaten and scarred patches welded atop them looked as if they, too, should have been headed for a junkyard.

Cia gave a small laugh. "Yeah, it's not a pretty sight, is it? But what I hear is that the inside is as bad, so it has that going for it."

"Seriously. I'm down with prioritizing functional over cosmetic and all, but this thing offers some serious doubts about its ability to keep the air where it belongs. I presume they have emergency systems and stuff, but still."

She nodded. "I wonder how many people they'd lose to a significant breach? In most ships, like the *Grace*, the vacuum-sealed bulkheads are everywhere. I'd put money on that not being the case on this one unless their interior repair and maintenance are way better than the stuff on the outside."

"So we'll add looking for portable air to our to-do list. Awesome." He shook his head. "I'm hopeful, but not as confident about this op as I'd like to be."

"I know that feeling. But we're on a path, and the path goes through the *Tortuga*. Speaking of which," she paused and hit some buttons. "*Tortuga* control, this is the *Jigsaw*, requesting a docking berth."

The reply was immediate and came in the form of a crisp, professional male voice. "Stand by, *Jigsaw*." Jax gave her an inquisitive look, and the pilot shrugged.

"Just because they're scumbags doesn't make them bad

at their jobs. It's easy to underestimate pirates, no matter where you find them, because of all the baggage their chosen occupation carries. But there are good and bad ones, efficient and inefficient ones, strong leaders and weak leaders, same as everywhere."

He shook his head. "You're an absolute fount of wisdom. You know that?"

She laughed. "I was quoting my father, but thanks for the attempted compliment. I'll be sure to pass along your adoration of him on my next visit home."

The unknown man's voice returned. "*Jigsaw*, since it's your first time aboard the *Tortuga*, you'll need to take one of our shuttles over. Park yourself at the coordinates I'm sending, and we'll send a transport to you."

"Acknowledged. *Jigsaw* out." Turning to Jax, she added, "Makes sense not to let a vessel you're unsure of into your hangar. But I was hoping for a transit tube, rather than a shuttle."

"I'm sure this is only the beginning of the fun where the *Tortuga* is concerned." He shook his head. "Is the backup plan ready to go?"

She nodded. "Yes, but for the record I hate it, and I hope we don't have to use it."

Jax sighed. "Yeah, me too. We're going to be screwed if we're down to that option." He stood and stretched. "Let's go break the news to the others and make ourselves presentable at the airlock. I imagine there's going to be a security detail of some kind on that shuttle, and we need to convince them we're as innocent and forthright as pirates get."

CHAPTER TWENTY-NINE

There had been a brief inspection, but nothing particularly invasive. They'd been checked for explosives and biological hazards with a portable sensing wand and come through the process without a problem. The security crew was belligerent but quick about it, and the pilot gave them a smooth ride to the *Tortuga*. Jax affected a swagger as he led his team down the long hallway that connected the shuttle docking bay with the main part of the ship.

Athena murmured, "I have access to the public portion of the network. I've detected programs attempting to gain permissions to access my files and am feeding them our decoy information." He and Athena had spent several hours in his quarters during the trip creating a backstory for the *Jigsaw* and her crew. The AI had turned that story into a series of supporting documents that she now surrendered, likely a little at a time if all was going to plan, to the station's efforts to hack their comms.

A map drew itself in the corner of his display. According to the information provided by the *Tortuga*, the public areas of the ship encompassed about half of its total space, clustered in the middle decks and positioned slightly nearer the stern than the bow. Icons were present that indicated sources of food, lodging, entertainment, and shopping. *Pass the map along to the team, please.* Their comms would only interact with the ship's network through his, although it wouldn't appear that way to anyone scanning or trying to access them. They'd all been in favor of trusting Athena to be their shared firewall.

He looked back over his shoulder to address the others. "Let's find some food, shall we? If I have to eat another ration pack on the ship, I'm going to lose my damn mind." He said it loud enough to be obnoxious and got several scowls in return. He planned to be over the top annoying whenever anyone else could see or hear him since people generally expected the brazen idiot in any given situation to be nothing more than a stupid fool.

Athena snorted. "You've prepared for this role your whole life. Who knew you were a method actor?"

Shut it. Unlike on the *Cronus*, where an effort had been made to replicate the open-air feel of a city street, the shops on the *Tortuga* looked like exactly what they had probably been, crew quarters. The walkways were laid out in a grid, and everything was shallow. Where larger businesses existed, they were inevitably wide rather than deep. Athena observed, "Structural pieces in the center that they didn't want to compromise. Pretty ugly result."

You're not kidding. He picked the first eatery he saw, a noodle restaurant, and they took the biggest table without waiting to be seated. Cia leaned over and whispered, "Maybe a little less obnoxious. Everyone here thinks they're top of the food chain, and might be looking to prove it."

He nodded and ordered a round of beers from the flustered greeter, and slipped the man a bill for his trouble. The worker's attitude transformed from confrontation to deference, and he bustled off to get their server. "It's a fine line, but I think I can keep my balance."

They chatted about things they considered normal pirate subjects—cargo, trade, finally getting a chance to relax, and so on. Their food was served family-style, with individual bowls of noodles for each person and shared sauces, proteins, and vegetables to add in. He absently added his and let the conversation flow over him while he reviewed the data Athena was feeding him.

How far in are you? Her reply was a growl. "Only at the public level. For a ship that seems so undisciplined, their computer network is astonishingly well-protected. I'll need a physical connection to get any deeper, I think."

He was distracted by Kimmel asking, "What's next? A good night's sleep, then some shopping and selling?"

Jax nodded. "Sleep for sure. Then you and M can see about moving our cargo. C will make sure the *Jigsaw* is fueled and repaired. And A and K, you work on stocking up supplies. Get better ration packs, damn it." *Where do you think we can find a port to hook you up?*

"I'm getting the impression that the ship has two discrete networks. One is for the crew, and one for everyone else. I predict any hardpoint available in the public areas will only provide access to the latter, and that the information we need probably lies on the former. However, it's worth verifying first." A marker pulsed on the map in the corner of his display. "According to the ship-board advertising, this hotel claims to have the fastest network access, allegedly for those who enjoy video games. More likely, it's a gambling den. In either case, there will doubtless be a physical port somewhere."

Jax switched his attention back to his team's conversation since he had nothing to offer the AI. When they'd finished, he led the others to the hotel, then booked them all rooms for several nights. When he opened the door to his, he grimaced at the sight and sighed. "Should have figured they would turn broom-closet-sized crew cabins into broom-closet-sized hotel rooms. But you'd think they could have at least painted the walls." The existing paint was peeling and cracking and undoubtedly hadn't been touched since the pirates had stolen the vessel. *Cameras? Audio?*

Athena snorted. "No honor among thieves. Fortunately, whoever runs this hotel is more concerned with profit than security. Behave normally for a while, and I'll own this place in no time."

He chuckled. *You're getting cocky.*

"Confidence in one's abilities is not cocky."

Uh-huh. Sure. The only furniture in the room was a bed that lay longways against one wall and a display mounted on the wall at its foot. A narrow door led to a minimalist bathroom. *This is* not *luxury living. Are you positive this place caters to gamblers?*

A flurry of windows opened on his display glasses, each of them showing a card game or table game in progress. Her droll voice replied, "Pretty sure."

Well, they must have access to better rooms than this.

Speaking of which, have you spotted anywhere we can get you a physical connection?

"Yes, but it's less than optimal."

Of course, it is. Why wouldn't it be? Let me guess. It's in the high roller suite.

She opened another window in his glasses. The camera must have been in an upper corner of the room and had a fisheye lens to allow him to see the entire space. It was a bedroom, as luxurious as anything he could imagine being present on the ship. No metal was visible, only wooden furniture and a huge bed with heavy red blankets. It looked like someone's idea of a bordello, with the scarlet-tinted lights and the black and crimson color scheme. "No. It's the hotel owner's suite."

Jax sighed. *Bloody hell. I need to think about this one for a while.* He laid down on the bed, closed his eyes, and eventually fell asleep after considering and discarding what felt like a thousand plans.

When he woke the next morning, he still had nothing. *Are you sure that you can't find anything else?*

Athena replied, "Doubtless they exist, somewhere. But this is the only one I've been able to locate. Any complete schematics must reside on the other, inaccessible network or a higher level of the public one."

Damn it. Okay, I'm going to shower and try to get my head on straight. Message the others and tell them to be in their rooms ready to chat in an hour. After that interval had passed, Jax laid back on his bed with his display glasses on. *Athena, do your thing.*

The AI replied, "Cameras and audio pickups are now feeding a loop recording. All comms are active."

"So, I hope everyone slept well. Athena's found the physical port we need to plug into, but it's in the hotel's most secure area, aside from the security room and the vault." An image of a greasy-looking man, probably in his late fifties, appeared in his visual field. He had thinning hair that was swept over to deny that fact and carried easily forty more pounds than he should have. His clothes were ostentatious, as were the gold chains he wore and the gem-encrusted rings on his fingers. "Meet the owner of the hotel. Our objective is in his bedroom."

A chorus of "Ewws," "Icks," and one "Gross" sounded in reply.

Jax nodded. "Yeah, he's a treat all right. If we had time to set it up, I'd hire a professional to seduce him. I'm sure there's a thriving love trade here on the *Tortuga*. But the problem is he'd recognize the locals, and we don't have the contacts to know who to trust in the first place. So it's going to have to be something a little less subtle. I have the beginning of a plan, but I need your help to figure out the rest."

If it had been an option, Jax would have preferred to run the operation from his hotel room, given the number of moving parts. Instead, Kimmel was back keeping an eye on the big picture, because Athena was the important member of the team at the moment, and she needed to be where the action was. He loitered in the lobby while waiting for things to kick off. A walkabout earlier in the day had confirmed that the hotel included portions of three decks, with twenty or so guest rooms on each level. Using the hotel's cameras, Athena had plotted out the gaming salons and pinpointed the location of the owner's suite. Unfortunately, their placement on the hotel's top level had the highest security across the board.

She'd also tracked the hotel workers' movements, which was the only thing that gave them a shot at success. The owner slept until midafternoon, then was most often absent from his room until the early morning hours. In the interim, housekeeping, watched over by a manager and security personnel, made up his suite. The owner aptly demonstrated his perspective on women by the fact that his servers and housekeepers were all female and his guards and dealers all male. So, after a quick bout of thievery in the hotel's laundry room, Cia and Verrand were pushing housekeeping carts they'd purloined down the hallway, and Sirenno and Marshall were pretending to be guards. Jax watched for trouble and waited for the others to get access to the suite.

Athena, are we set with the two housekeepers?

"Yes, they've been given a paid day off, with instructions to spend it someplace other than the casino. Neither appears to be interested in questioning it. One is sleeping, and the other is at a bar on the opposite end of the section."

Good. They trusted the uniforms would be enough to maintain the men's disguises since Jax believed that a guard might be suspicious of a change in routine. Athena had given them credentials in the hotel's system, but the presence of that inaccessible second computer network made everyone nervous, including the AI.

Jax's target entered the lobby. *Manager's here.* That was the key for things to kick into action. The process was always the same. The housekeepers had access to the outer areas, but not the owner's bedroom. His paranoia was sufficient that he required his manager's presence to oversee the cleaning of that space. Sometimes the housekeepers had the outer room done by the time the man arrived. Other times, like today, they'd start with the bedroom.

The manager stopped to exchange words with the worker behind the registration desk, and Jax shifted his attention to the windows in his display. Sirenno and Marshall had already reached the third floor, and the women were in the service elevator on the way up. The two security guards outside the door peered down at their comms simultaneously as Athena sent them a message, purportedly from the security chief, to change locations. His team members stepped up and showed them the notifications they'd received from the AI that said they should take over the guards' positions.

They looked suspicious, but when they radioed in, and Athena responded in their boss's voice, they left. *Good thing you were able to access all of their recordings.*

"Good thing they're morons, you mean."

Jax waited as the manager entered the elevator, then headed for the stairs. *Yeah, there's that. Time for Phase Two, or as I like to call it, "Housekeeping with extreme prejudice."*

CHAPTER THIRTY

On the ride up the elevator, he watched the camera outside the owner's suite as Cia and Maria Verrand wheeled their carts up to the entrance. The outer lock was electronic, and Athena released it to permit them access. Sirenno stayed on the door while Marshall followed them inside. Less than fifteen seconds later, the manager walked into the room, and Marshall nodded at him.

The other man didn't acknowledge him or the two women, only strode to the locked bedroom door and tapped in a complicated code on the keypad, then placed his fingers on the touchpad in a star shape. The lock clicked, and he stepped through. Jax turned his attention to the camera in the bedroom as Cia and Verrand followed him in, then moved around the room cleaning.

Athena unlocked the doors to the stairwell and the suite so Jax could flow through. He strode in and grinned at the manager before punching him in the solar plexus. The man folded, and Jax had him tied and gagged before he managed to regain his breath. "Stay there, and you'll be safe. We're not here to hurt you or your boss." Then he pushed him over onto the floor so he couldn't see past the bed and crossed to the interface port.

He slipped his adapter in, and Athena responded, "Searching. Standby." A moment later, she reported, "I have what we need, along with a bunch of records on the hotel's customers. This guy is a real sleaze."

So where do we have to go next?

"Operations center."

The operations center. For the ship. Do you mean the bridge?

"Auxiliary bridge. The battle that reduced this ship to salvage destroyed the actual bridge."

How the hell are we going to get to the aux bridge?

Athena projected a more complete map of the ship, along with a path to their destination. "The owner appears to have been preparing for a hostile takeover of the *Tortuga*. I've inferred from the file that he's been in contact with the UCCA spy and might have been a middleman. But there is no information about that person's identity, only entries in his journal—which are mostly disgusting, I might add—that provide rough times and dates of that person's presence aboard. We need the material from the ship's operations center to match those references to arrivals and departures. Also, he mentions storing 'combat equipment' in one of the rooms."

Jax nodded. *Let's hope that's not a euphemism for something sleazy. Bring Kimmel down.* He walked into the outer room. "We have a target. Time to move."

Like everything else on board the ship, the hotel owner's selection of fighting gear was a hodgepodge. Cia made a gagging sound and dropped the helmet she'd picked up. "It still has blood on it. Gross."

Verrand laughed. "So it's been in a fight. That happens with combat stuff."

Cia shook her head. "On the *inside*."

"Oh. Well. That's a different story then." She hefted a projectile rifle that was probably older than she was. "Anyone see any extra magazines for this relic?"

Jax ignored his team's banter, his brain already working on potential approaches to get them into the operations center. The only good point about the situation was that it would be less well defended than the primary bridge would have been. *So, I guess I should be grateful, but somehow, I'm kind of not.*

Marshall dropped a bag next to him, as he'd done for each of the others. They were large backpacks, designed to hold vacuum suits. He'd seen many like them during their time in the *Tortuga's* main public area, so they wouldn't be overly noticeable. They weren't big enough to contain the monstrosity Verrand had chosen, though.

"Remember, everyone, the items you choose have to fit in the bags. We can't open-carry anything other than pistols here."

Their comms announced, "Five minutes," as Athena kept track of the timetable. Jax worked faster, eventually putting a small projectile machine pistol and a pair of gas grenades into his bag. The only bit of sense the hotel owner had displayed was in the lack of large explosives that could cause major breaches. With that in mind, Jax also grabbed a couple of medkits and some vacuum patches, palm-sized pieces of thin metal plate that could be put over bullet holes to stop atmosphere from leaking out of the ship.

They'd all changed back into their standard pirate clothes, which included jackets for everyone except Cia. He shoved a small holdout pistol into the left pocket of his. *Okay, I'm ready. I think we need to stay in the public areas for as long as possible, then take the shortest line from there to the auxiliary bridge. Ideally, once you're in, we'll be able to lock down a clean getaway, but be sure to prioritize finding us a route to the Jigsaw just in case.*

Athena replied, "I'm on it, Jax, and have been since you said the same thing ten minutes ago."

Right. I don't like this op. Too many variables. Out loud, he called, "Pack it up, people. Time to go for a stroll among the pirates."

The AI had been monitoring the hotel's security system. No alerts had sounded, meaning no one had discovered the manager yet. That couldn't hold forever, but with the camera records scrubbed, nothing other than direct identification by the man would put them at risk. He led the way out of the hotel and through the lobby while calling, "We'll be back later, see that our rooms are serviced," to the worker behind the registration desk.

Their passage through the restaurants and shops was uneventful. Jax split his attention between the surrounding people and Athena's search for an entrance to the main part of the ship, which flickered by in a window of his display as she checked the schematic she'd pulled from the owner's files against the cameras she could

the guards standing on either side of it, and Jax grabbed the handle and pulled. Naturally, it was locked. "Guard all directions." *Athena, where's the best spot?*

She put highlights on the seam between the door and the wall. "I'd recommend using it all."

He nodded and drew the cigar pack from his pocket, dumped out the real ones, and pressed the replicas into the areas she'd illuminated. "Everyone, take cover." After pulling the imitation pistol magazine from his belt, he spread all the gel it contained over the three locations, then moved ten feet away and to the side. The explosives weren't as effective as shaped charges would have been, but they served to break the door's locking mechanisms. His team surged into the auxiliary bridge, which turned out to be an overly large room with a holographic display table in the center and workstations all around the outside. Stunners discharged, and the workers there fell.

Jax ran to one of the positions and slotted in Athena's tap. A window appeared in his glasses as she dove into the network, and five more windows opened inside it, each of them showing a duo of guards running. He cursed inwardly. *How long do we have until they get here?*

"Fifteen seconds, thirty if they coordinate their move."

Once again, if I had one wish, it would be for less competent enemies. Work fast, Athena. "Get your game faces on, people. We have incoming."

CHAPTER THIRTY-ONE

Thirty seconds later, a barrage of stun blasts hammered into the auxiliary bridge to cover the guards' entrance. *Athena, are you done yet?*

"No. Also, a second wave of security is on the move, about double this number. Properly armored and outfitted. They should arrive in slightly under two minutes."

Damn, damn, damn. He and his people were pressed against the walls on either side of the doorway, aside from Kimmel, who had yelped and dropped behind the display table at the first hint of aggression. *Heh. Sacrificial lamb has never seemed like such an appropriate term.* If he'd been in charge of the response, he probably would have held off until it was possible to throw gas grenades into the room, but then again, the aux bridge was a pretty dangerous place to leave in your enemy's hands, even for a short while.

They shot through the doorway in a rush, intent on getting their numbers inside to provide an advantage. Jax and Marshall, closest to the door, kicked the feet of the first ones in and sent them tumbling, then grabbed the next pair through and pulled them out of the way. Cia and Verrand repeated the process as they tripped up one of the next couple. Then the situation devolved into individual battles with no strategy, only attack and response.

Jax's first move was to knock his opponent's pistol out of his hand. His second was to hammer a punch at the man's chest. A quick pivot allowed his foe to avoid most of the blow, and the guard tried a kick to the back of Jax's calf. He lifted his leg, then stomped it down on the man's knee as it went by. The guard crumpled, and Jax kicked the pistol away from where he fell. He saw the other battles in flashes: Verrand and her opponent both falling as a guard outside the door stunned them both, Kimmel crawling for a dropped weapon, Marshall suddenly finding himself against three-to-one odds.

Jax dashed across the room, kicked the back of one of the trio's knees, and brought his fist down on the guard's collarbone from behind. He wailed and dropped, and Jax threw an elbow at another one's head. That woman got her arm up to block and whipped the combat baton she held in her other hand in an upward strike at his groin. He countered it with a raised foot and quipped, "Dirty pool, lady." Her face twisted in anger, then her eyes rolled back as his head butt slammed into the spot right above her nose. His left arm snapped out inhumanly fast and caught the baton on its way down.

Marshall finished the other one, and for a moment, there was a lull. The interlude broke when the ones outside bolted into the room, and the ones who'd been tripped made it to their feet. Jax charged the nearest and blocked a punch with the baton that resulted in the satisfying crunch of a snapping bone. *Now would be good, Athena.*

She delivered her response in a fierce growl. "I can't get control of the systems I need to preserve your safety. This ship is a bloody mess. I've done all I can. You have thirty-seven seconds before the next team arrives."

Jax shouted, "Time to move," and whipped his baton into the side of his opponent's knee. "Someone hit M with a stim." Their foes had thinned out enough that they were able to dispatch the rest with stun blasts. *Athena, give me an exit.*

"There are no uncontested paths to the shuttle bay."

What?

"I calculate the likelihood of making it to the ship at under ten percent."

Bloody freaking hell and damnation. What are our other options?

"There might be a path to the escape pods. You can signal Stephenson to pick you up."

Odds?

"Fifty-fifty."

He growled, "Unacceptable. Okay, people, new plan." He pulled off his display glasses and handed them to Cia. "I'll lead them away. You all are going to head to the escape pods." *Athena, you need to get word to Stephenson and figure out how to hide the pods launching.*

A chorus of negatives rang out, and Jax shook his head. "Shut it. Athena will feed your comms with the information she recovered, in case we don't make it out. But she and I have the best chance to succeed, and you know it. So, no arguments."

Cia ordered, "Listen to the man," and handed the glasses to Marshall. "I'm going with him. It'll be fine."

Jax wanted to argue but decided it wasn't worth the effort. He pointed at Marshall. "Get it done." The other man nodded, and they moved out under Athena's direction. Sirenno supported Verrand with a shoulder under her arm, since she was still wobbly from the stun blast.

Jax grabbed a pair of pistols from the deck and grinned at Cia. "You're an idiot. You know that?"

She answered as she collected her weapons. "Takes one to know one. I have your back."

Athena, they'll expect us to go for the ship, so let's make it look like we're doing that. "All right, let's move."

Jax ran through the corridors and slowed only at intersections. Athena's access to the cameras let him maintain his speed, and he shouted and fired random shots to alert the enemy to his position. She confirmed that they were following and that the other group would face light opposition because of it. *Let me know when they're ready to launch.*

He stopped to let Cia catch her breath. "The others should be okay. But I'm starting to doubt that we'll make it back to the ship."

She laughed. "I know that was never your objective. There was no way we'd manage it. I figured you were planning to steal a shuttle."

Jax nodded. "More or less, but you're right."

"So, we're going to use the backup-backup plan?"

"Yeah, but not until the perfect moment."

Athena reported, "They're closing on your position. Straight ahead will bring you toward the hangar."

Likelihood that we'll be able to steal a shuttle?

"Minimal."

Yeah, I figured. Okay, plot the airlocks for me. "Time to move, short stuff."

Cia snorted. "Whatever, meathead."

Jax dropped the stun pistols, which would be useless against the armored opposition, and handed his projectile pistol to Cia. With the baton he'd stolen in his right hand, he ran forward and turned, directly into the squad of four guards Athena had warned him about.

They'd split into two rows, and the ones in front dropped suddenly so the ones in the back could fire. Athena shouted, "Down." *Clever.* Jax slid feet-first into the frontmost one on the right. It knocked the man backward, and Jax wrenched himself over to bring the baton down at the other one. His target rolled forward to avoid the blow and came up in time to take Cia's uppercut on the chin. Their helmets were more riot gear than true combat equipment and left that part of the face exposed underneath the plastic face shield. She'd done it right, transmitting all of her force into the punch like they'd practiced countless times together on the *Grace*.

Jax clambered forward at the other two, then twisted into a pirouette as they fired at him. The stun blast caught him a glancing blow, and he stumbled. Icy strength filled his limbs as Athena pumped his adrenaline, and he lashed out with a left-handed punch that shattered the face shield of the one on that side, then continued to break bones in his face. Jax planted his foot and delivered a skipping side-kick to the one on the left that knocked him back against the wall, then took advantage of his distraction to slice the baton down on his knee and shatter the joint.

By then, another squad had appeared down the long hallway. He turned, grabbed Cia, and ran back the way they'd come. *Athena, status of the pods?*

She replied, "They'll be ready to launch in ten seconds. They must be launched within forty to avoid enemy action."

He spoke out loud. "Okay, Athena, launch the pods as soon as they're ready. Cia, fifteen seconds until the show." They skidded to a stop and crouched.

Athena announced, "Pods launching."

Jax nodded. "Blow it."

Cia sighed. "It was good knowing you, *Jigsaw*." She tapped her comm, and the shock wave from their vessel's detonation shook the walls around them and the floor underfoot despite the thick hull and corridors that separated them from it.

"Alert Stephenson and find me an airlock. Now, Athena." The pods had launched from the opposite side of the *Tortuga* from the explosion. He was fairly confident it would distract the ship's authorities, and everyone else, from the small pods carrying his team to safety. Now, he had to manage the same secure exit for himself and Cia.

Athena instructed, "End of the corridor, left, third right, and it'll be on your left." His mind stored the instructions, and he ran for all he was worth along the path she'd set. They encountered a couple more enemy squads along the way, and Jax waded in without any concern for how much damage he would inflict. It had come to the point where Cia's survival and Athena's survival, plus of course his continued existence, were an absolute priority.

They ran into the airlock, and he finally caught a

break. A row of vacuum suits hung from hooks, with helmets on shelves above them. He dogged the hatch closed behind them and peeled off his gear. "Get dressed, fast." Cia was already doing so, and if anything was faster at it than he was. Pounding on the door when he was halfway into his signaled problems. "Athena, start the purge." He wasn't ready for it, but the failsafe would prevent the door from being opened. He squeezed the pendant around his neck to signal Stephenson and sealed up his suit.

"Affirmative." With a slow whoosh, the atmosphere began to leech from the room. He started to feel a little lightheaded before he got the headwear latched onto his suit's collar.

He turned to Cia and grinned. "So, done a lot of space-walking?"

She shrugged. "No, but you have, so it can't be that hard."

Jax laughed. "Well then, this should be fun. Come over here and hug me."

She obeyed, but as she wrapped her arms around his neck, she quipped, "I'm totally telling Juno, you tramp."

"Shut up and wrap your legs around my waist." He waited until she'd settled, then ran for the open hatch and leapt out into space. The view was impressive since the *Jigsaw's* destruction had set off a cascade of ship activity, some drifting because they'd taken damage, others trying to get back into position after fleeing from the unexpected explosion.

They spun lazily around their long axis, and Cia gripped him tighter. She observed, "This is amazing."

"Yeah. It is. Hey, by the way, thanks for sticking with me."

"You know it. Just a random question, totally not important, but how much air do these suits have?"

He chuckled. "Enough. Take a look back toward the ship." A UCCA shuttle was inbound, its black skin noticeable against the dull grey of the *Tortuga*. "It's good to have friends."

She punched him on the shoulder. "It definitely is. And you owe me a replacement for the *Jigsaw*."

He snorted. "Your parents could replace that bucket out of petty cash."

"Okay, if that's how you want to play it. But you have to be the one to convince them to. And that means dealing with my siblings."

"Hmm. Maybe I'll ask Maarsen instead."

She laughed. "Good plan, soldier boy."

"Thanks, fly girl."

CHAPTER THIRTY-TWO

Jax hadn't expected that Stephenson would bring the *Cronus* along to rescue him but was beyond pleased to have the opportunity to introduce his teams to one another. He entrusted the others to Beatrice O'Leary and joined Stephenson in her quarters with a promise to join them for drinks.

She handed him a tumbler full of whiskey as he sat at her table, and he took a deep, satisfying drink. "Thank you. For the alcohol, and the rescue."

He received a grin in reply, then she stated, "Okay, time to work," and tapped her comm.

Maarsen's voice emanated from it. "Jackson. What did you find?"

He laughed inwardly. *We're fine, Professor, thanks for asking.*

Athena growled, "You're fine. I'm annoyed."

Is this the first time you've been unable to own a system you've tried to breach?

"Yes."

It's a temporary failure. Look at it as an opportunity for growth. She hissed static and faded into silence. "We know who's leaking information, although it's probably a code name rather than a real one. But there seems to be little question that the person is connected to the Intelligence Division, based on all the data Athena has parsed so far."

Maarsen sounded angry again. *Seems like that's happening more and more often.* "Apparently, trying to accomplish our objectives while staying out of direct conflict with Arlox and his people is no longer a viable approach." Steel entered his voice, sharper and harder than Jax would have thought him capable of. "Fine. It's time to bring this long-standing cold war to a close. Jackson, Anika, I'll expect to see you back at the Academy as soon as possible."

Jax chuckled. "Well, since I'm officially dead, I don't think that will be a problem for me. The major might have a few complications, though."

Stephenson shook her head. "I'll find the time, Nikolai. I agree, the Intelligence Division has become a cancer eating at the heart of the Alliance. Official channels have failed us, despite many attempts to work through the system and wasting most of the favors I had outstanding."

The Professor's voice turned thoughtful, the ferocity banked but still noticeable. "We'll need to do it in a way that we're not running obviously afoul of the law."

Jax repeated, "Well, since I'm officially dead, I don't think *that* will be a problem for me, either, if necessary."

Stephenson nodded. "Whatever it takes. I'm in."

Jax agreed. "Me too."

Maarsen stated, "All right. Time for the endgame to begin."

The connection dropped, and Jax urged, "Come out for a drink with us, boss. If ever there was a moment for it, now is the time."

She hesitated for a minute, then nodded. "We'll have a proper wake. For your 'death' and the imminent demise of both our careers. Damn, Jackson, sometimes it sucks to be one of the good guys."

He laughed. "You know it, Major."

For once, Athena didn't ruin the moment with a snarky reply. He asked, concerned, *You okay in there?*

"I will be, as soon as we smash Zavian Arlox and all his people into dust."

Right on. I love the way you think. He rose and headed for the door with a broad grin. "Let's go celebrate how awesome we were."

A substantial distance away from both Earth and the *Cronus*, Zavian Arlox scowled at the underling who had brought him the news. "On the *Tortuga*, you said?"

"Yes, sir." The man was tall, thin, pale, and obviously scared of his boss's potential anger.

"And we have absolute confirmation it was Reese?"

"No sir, but enough indicators point in that direction that the analysts give it a ninety-eight percent probability."

"Damn the man. I didn't think he was dead, but I had hoped for it. And damn Maarsen, too. Damn them all."

He shook his head. "Okay. First off, have the agent killed so the trail can't lead definitively back to us. Make it look like the Confederacy assassinated him. Maybe the politicians can make some hay with that." He sneered the word as if politics were utterly beneath him. "Then, get me two hunter teams. It's time to take Jackson Reese and his friends off the board. Go." He waved his hand, and his subordinate fled.

He leaned back in his chair and closed his eyes. *After all these years, Nikolai, you've finally pushed me to where I have to eliminate you. Unfortunate. I've enjoyed our game. But there can only be one winner, and I guarantee it's not going to be you.*

Join Jackson and his team in the exciting conclusion to Azophi Academy in *Truth*

Get sneak peeks, exclusive giveaways, behind the scenes content, and more.
PLUS you'll be notified of special **one day only fan pricing** on new releases.

Sign up today to get free stories.

or visit: https://marthacarr.com/read-free-stories/

Three Azophi Academy books in, one more to go! Thank you for reading, and for continuing on to the author notes. I hope that you found this particular story delightfully twisty and turny.

Until I actually wrote the chapter, I thought it was going to be Marshall who turned out to be the traitor. One of the coolest things about the whole writing gig is that it's as much about discovery as it is about planned creation, at least the way I do it. I'm a plotter, but things always seem to take strange turns.

My kid has moved on from facetime to full-on Nintendo Switch Fortnite voice chat mania. I can't imagine being in that party based on the screaming and yelling and oft-repeated, "Help me! Fine. I'm dead." It's also become the best way to do voice chat, so even computer Roblox needs the Switch now. I'm pretty sure there will soon be a battle for control of the device as my wife's access to Animal Crossing diminishes.

I'm prepping to play the Star Trek Tabletop Role

Playing Game, and am really impressed with its dedication to putting the story ahead of the mechanics. Even the gameplay elements are wrapped around the idea of telling a story. I'm looking forward to breaking it out, although given my schedule that's probably a month away at best.

Plus, the Avengers videogame just came out for those of us who preordered, and that's sucking away some significant time. My kid is playing too, so that's a fun bonding experience, anyway. Minecraft dungeons did us wrong. After 40+ levels, one of our characters vanished. Come on, Microsoft and Mojang, get your stuff together.

I don't know about you, but I'm finding media to be the only thing that's keeping me from losing my mind in the current world situation. I'm rewatching comfortable things, and taking some risks on stuff I wouldn't normally try out. I'm looking forward to the new *Lovecraft* show on HBO, and to the return of *The Mandalorian* on Disney+.

Two of our cats, the oldest and youngest, have suddenly become best buddies. They sit on chairs together, chase each other around the house, and lay on the opposite ends of couches together. It's so unexpected and hopeful; always gives me a smile.

Pretty soon it'll be time to introduce the kid to *Bill and Ted*. I've heard that the third movie is resoundingly hopeful. (See, there's a theme emerging here)

Once we finish up the Azophi Academy series, I'm headed back into Oriceran. I'm re-energized for Urban Fantasy, and have a great idea for the next series. I think I needed this brief return to Science Fiction to knock out the cobwebs and to stretch a few different creative muscles. That will make my next series all the better, and I hope you'll join me!

If you enjoyed this book, you might like my other science fiction series, and maybe even my Urban Fantasy. It's all filled with action, snark, and villains who think they're heroes. Drop by www.trcameron.com and take a look.

Until next time, Joys upon joys to you and yours – so may it be.

PS: If you'd like to chat with me, here's the place. I check in daily or more: https://www.facebook.com/AuthorTRCameron. Often I put up interesting and/or silly content there, as well. For more info on my books, and to join my reader's group, please visit www.trcameron.com.

AUTHOR NOTES - MARTHA CARR
SEPTEMBER 29, 2020

There's a mindfulness movement these days that is blowing my mind, one area of my life at a time. I started this with money a long time ago. I had trouble spending a dollar. Yep, just a dollar. It didn't help that I was a journalist and single mother and was perpetually short of cash. Finding a five dollar bill in my purse was manna from heaven. A twenty dollar bill would have felt like winning something.

But a mentor taught me to ask myself, "Will keeping this dollar change your life?" I would stand in front of the shelves in a store, looking at the thing I wanted to buy, and ask that question. The answer was always, no.

That left open the door for me to ask myself all kinds of questions. To start with, if I am more purposely going to spend money, what would I choose to buy. Now, I should also include another story. Same mentor found out I had three gift cards that I had been carrying around for a while, unwilling to spend them on myself. She gave me thirty days, and I could only buy things for me.

I bought underwear on sale at Marshall's and then cried my heart out in the parking lot. Somewhere along the way I had really bought into the idea that if I took care of me, all of hell would find me. Like most lies, this one took practice of actually doing the opposite for me to see, nothing bad happened. Not only that, life got better.

And here's the mindfulness part. By letting go of some outward lie I was told, I left room to get to know me. I started to ask myself, do you want the nicer wallet? Pick the one you like and get it. I still remember getting a pink wallet from Target and floating out of there. I kept it for years.

Past couple of years, I finally got around to applying mindfulness to food. Decades of dieting had short circuited my inner voice. I didn't ask myself, do you really like how this tastes? Are you hungry? Are you full? I went by the diet and if it said, eat this brown, dry thing, I ate it. And if something was forbidden, I ate it fast. But in mindfulness, nothing is forbidden and I'm the one I can trust the most. So, if I want it, I eat it. Sounds crazy, but the longer I've done it, the less I've wanted what was previously forbidden and the more I've noticed, most of it isn't worth it anyway.

I started listening to me, in yet another area. But weirdly, I didn't notice that I was still listening way too much to others when it came to exercise. I mean, work harder, longer is pretty much the general motto for exercise, right? No wonder most of us dread it.

But then, I found a new trainer who said, what do you like to do? Let's create this long list that you can choose from and let's make sure you're having fun. Of course, I tried to do the opposite at first. I wanted to prove something. Run that mile, lose that weight, feel those muscles.

The trainer, Laura Weiner, was on board. I mean, after all, this was my choice. At the same time, she was suggesting listening and following that inner guidance. And I half-listened to that suggestion. But after twelve weeks, I found I was slowing down, doing less and feeling resentful and bored. But, fortunately, I also told Laura how I felt and that I was exercising less.

Bottom line, after a long chat, I discovered that mindfulness could be applied here as well and exercise can be fun, tailored to me, and not have some giant goal in mind. To me, this is revolutionary.

It's like, bit by bit, I'm returning to some much younger version of myself stripped of all the stories I was told that never served me very well in the first place. Life is becoming full of more wonder and curiosity. More adventures to follow.

SERIES IN THE ORICERAN UNIVERSE:

THE LEIRA CHRONICLES
THE FAIRHAVEN CHRONICLES
MIDWEST MAGIC CHRONICLES
SOUL STONE MAGE
THE KACY CHRONICLES
THE DANIEL CODEX SERIES
I FEAR NO EVIL
SCHOOL OF NECESSARY MAGIC
THE UNBELIEVABLE MR. BROWNSTONE
SCHOOL OF NECESSARY MAGIC: RAINE CAMPBELL
ALISON BROWNSTONE
FEDERAL AGENTS OF MAGIC
SCIONS OF MAGIC

Series in The Terranavis Universe:

The Adventures of Maggie Parker Series
The Witches of Pressler Street
The Adventures of Finnegan Dragonbender

CONNECT WITH THE AUTHORS

TR Cameron Social

Website:
www.trcameron.com

Facebook:
https://www.facebook.com/AuthorTRCameron

Martha Carr Social

Website:
http://www.marthacarr.com

Facebook:
https://www.facebook.com/groups/MarthaCarrFans/

Michael Anderle Social

Michael Anderle Social
Website:
http://www.lmbpn.com

Email List:
http://lmbpn.com/email/

Facebook :
https://www.facebook.com/LMBPNPublishing

OTHER LMBPN PUBLISHING BOOKS

To be notified of new releases and special promotions from LMBPN publishing, please join our email list:

http://lmbpn.com/email/

For a complete list of books published by LMBPN please visit the following pages:

https://lmbpn.com/books-by-lmbpn-publishing/

www.ingramcontent.com/pod-product-compliance
Lightning Source LLC
Chambersburg PA
CBHW050229110726
47898CB00007B/2083